THE PURSUIT OF COCONUTS

CHRISTOPHER SHEVLIN

ALBATROSS

1

WAKING UP

There was soft sand beneath his cheek and fingertips. He was lying on his side, warm saliva pooling at the corner of his mouth, trailing down his cheek. The sun's heat glowed pleasantly on the back of his hand. He was entirely and beautifully rested, as though he had drunk a cool bowlful of sleep.

He opened his eyes, just a crack, and noticed there was a cotton hat over most of his face, so all he could see was a small patch of golden sand and an olive-green sleeve. His lazy attempt to roll over was hampered by a small but solidly packed rucksack strapped to his back. This amused him. He didn't know why.

After some fumbling, he managed to steer his

sleepy limbs into a sitting position, propped up against his rucksack and the gentle upward curve of the beach. He looked around.

In front of him stretched a sea of almost overpoweringly deep and shining green, its waves overlaid by silver glints. The white-gold sun stood tall in a sky of perfect blue, with a small fleet of clouds bunched on the far horizon. Off to either side of him ran creamy sand, as though freshly poured. He turned to look behind him, moving freely, with no trace of stiffness or discomfort. There he saw a collection of pleasingly squat and sturdy trees, trunks glowing red-brown and leaves shining green. A long way beyond and above the trees was a mountain, green on its lower reaches and turning lavender-grey nearer the summit.

There was no other person to be seen.

He stood. He was alone and had no idea where he was, or how he came to be there, and yet he felt calm and relaxed. A sense of perfect wellness glowed in every part of his body.

'Better take a look around,' he said. And then he laughed, because the sun and sand just smiled blankly back at him, clearly feeling no reply was needed.

He walked towards the trees. The sun was

warm, but there was a slight breeze, so he was completely comfortable in his light boots, cotton trousers and jacket. As he reached the first tree, he patted its solid trunk, feeling the living wood beneath his fingers. On the ground between the trees were leafy shrubs, vines and occasional flowers, mixed pale and vivid. He stepped in, past the first tree, drawn by the cool darkness. After passing a few more red-brown trees, he reached a clearer area where the sunlight fell in. Here he spotted a palm tree, and at its base a coconut. He walked through the sunlight, picked up the smooth green ball and found that he was thirsty.

'I'd give anything to be able to get into this thing and drink the milk,' he told the tree. Then he remembered the rucksack on his back. He took it off, squatted down and carefully unzipped it.

There was a light grey-blue blanket, neatly folded and warm to the touch. There was a waterproof sheet, also neatly folded and in its own plastic case. There was a pouch containing a net, with ropes and shiny carabiners. There was a metal travel stove and a wind-up torch. There was more, but he stopped investigating when he discovered a fabric case of tools, which included a short metal tube with a wooden handle on one end.

Somehow, he knew exactly what to do. He held the coconut firmly between his thighs, pushed the metal tube against its top and turned the handle. After a couple of turns, a corkscrew inside gripped the coconut, forcing the metal tube into it. With a few more twists of the handle there was a hollow *thunk* sound, and resistance ceased. When he pulled out the tool, he saw that the coconut had a neat hole in it, easily big enough to insert the metal drinking straw that was also in the tool case. He sucked down the cool, slightly sweet liquid inside. When he had finished, he leaned back against the palm tree to take stock of his situation.

His eyes flicked open. He must have fallen asleep. There was a soft crashing sound behind him, the sort of noise a very clumsy person might make when creeping through a forest. He remained perfectly still.

Someone emerged into the clearing and stopped, facing away from him, towards the sea.

'Oh my *God*, the *ocean,*' said a woman's voice. 'Would you take a look at that.'

She was short and stick-thin, wearing light boots, blue trousers and an olive-green jacket, all just like his own. A shapeless beige sunhat was balanced on top of tightly curled reddish hair that exploded from both sides of her head, as though reaching out for the trees. On her back was a rucksack like his.

'Quite a sight,' he said.

She spun around, her wide-open eyes seeming to jangle around in her large glasses.

'Oh my God!' she said. 'Who *are* you? I mean *hello*. But who *are* you?'

'I…' He stopped, surprised at realising something he should have noticed before. 'I have no idea. Not a clue.'

'You don't *know* who you *are?*'

'I woke up on the beach a few minutes ago. I guess I forgot.'

'You *forgot?*'

'I just said so, didn't I?'

His voice sounded loud, a little angry, and the woman was wringing her hands, an apprehensive look in her eyes.

There was a silence. And then a little more silence.

Finally, the woman said, 'You think maybe you're a *Peter?* You look like a Peter.'

'I don't know. I told you.'

'Well I think you'd be a Peter.'

'Fine,' he said. 'I'm a Peter. Anything for a quiet life. So, what's your name?'

'I...' She fell silent.

'You don't know either?'

She shook her head.

'You can be Doris.'

'*Doris!* What have I done that you call me *Doris?*'

'Fine. Angela then.'

'*Angela!* My God. What *am* I, a middle-aged lady with frizzy hair?'

'I hate to be the one to break it to you, but yes, I'd say that's exactly what you are.'

She looked at him through her large glasses, eyes wide. Then she touched her hair, said, '*Well!*' and turned her back on him.

'Fine,' he said. 'Sulk at me. See if I care.'

She didn't move.

'You know what,' he said. 'Why don't you tell me what I look like? It'll make you feel better.'

She slowly turned around and looked him up

and down. He took off his hat and she appraised him.

'You know what you look like?' she said. 'A shaved melon.'

'Fine. I don't think you see too many hairy melons, but fine.'

'That had a *hard* life.'

'I can take that.'

'And you got too much hair around your ears and big bags under your eyes. And my God you look *harsh*. Real harsh.'

'Yeah, well you look like your hair just got a look at your face and decided to get away as fast as possible.'

She took a sharp breath and turned her back again. He folded his arms and reclined forcefully against the palm tree, making its fronds shake. They remained that way for a few moments, and then something heavy hit Angela's rucksack and fell to the ground beside her with a thud. She spun around.

'What, now you're *throwing* things at me?'

'I didn't throw anything.'

'You did *so*. I felt it.'

'It's a coconut, Angela. It fell from the tree.'

She looked down at it, unwilling to believe him.

'You thirsty?' he asked. 'It's got milk inside.'

She hesitated.

'What do I do with it?' she asked, picking it up suspiciously.

'Look in your backpack, Angela.'

She took off her rucksack and opened it.

'What am I looking *for*?'

'One of these.' He held up his tool pouch. 'It's in the front compartment … No, the *front* compartment. That's it, Angela.'

'Am I ever sorry I gave you a nice name, Peter. I can't *believe* you made me an Angela.'

'You got one of these?' he asked, holding up his coconut tool.

'No!'

She threw the tool pouch at him. He picked it up and looked through it.

'Hey,' he said. 'You got different tools.'

'So what am I supposed to do about *that?*'

'Pass me the coconut, Angela. I'll use my doohickey on it.'

'Are you hungry, Peter?'

He'd been asleep again. Now he was flailing

back into wakefulness as Angela prodded his shoulder with an empty coconut. The great sense of calm wellbeing was almost gone. He felt raw and ragged, like an undercooked egg.

'What?' he said.

'I *said*, are you hungry?'

'To sleep is to dine, Angela. I was fine till you woke me.'

'*To sleep is to dine*. Where's *that* from?'

'How would I know? I don't even know my real name. Maybe I just made it up. Maybe my mom sang it to me in my cradle. Maybe I have it tattooed on my ass cheeks. I have no clue.'

They were silent for a while. Peter stood up. It was a little cooler, though still pleasantly warm, and the sun hung lower in the sky.

'So. You hungry?' Angela asked again.

'Yes, I'm hungry.'

'What do you wanna eat?'

'What do I want to eat? You make it sound like we're in a restaurant. I want a beef bourguignon! I want truffles and canapés and caviar! We're on a desert island for Chrissakes. What have we got?'

'Coconuts.'

'Right. But how do we open them? We've drunk

the milk. How do we eat the … the whatever it's called? Meat? We've only got the corkscrew.'

'I don't *know*, Peter.'

'I don't know either, Angela.'

He sat down.

'Wait. You hear that?' he said.

'What?'

'That *noise*, Angela. What else would you hear?'

'What noise?'

'Shh!'

There was a muffled crashing of undergrowth.

'Hello!' he called.

There was no reply, but the crashing grew louder and nearer.

'Hello!' Angela called in a high, wavering voice.

Peter stood up and looked around. 'I need a stick.'

'What for?'

Whatever was coming through the undergrowth was just a few yards away by now, though they couldn't see it. The sound was coming from the place where the trees were thickest and the forest most dark.

'What for? In case that sound's a goddamn … lion or something. I am not going to wind up being eaten on my first day in this place.'

He picked up a stick, but it was too long and thin to use as a weapon.

'Have you got the coconut corkscrew, Angela?'

Crash. Crash. Crash.

'You are not going to fight a *lion* with a coconut corkscrew, Peter!'

'Well I've got to fight it with something, for Chrissakes! It's almost on top of us.'

'Oh my God!'

And then out into the clearing walked a short, tubby man wearing glasses, with brown curly hair encircling his bald, pink head. He was dressed exactly like Peter and Angela, and he was eating a mango, which he held in both his chubby hands. The lower half of his face shone with the juice.

Peter and Angela stared at him, open-mouthed. The tubby man looked at them short-sightedly, adjusted his glasses and took another bite. A speck of mango flesh clung to the edge of one of his lenses.

'Hi. Didn't you hear us? We were shouting "Hello."'

'I didn't know you were talking to me,' said the tubby man.

'You frightened us half to–' began Angela.

'You didn't know we were talking to you? Who

the hell else are we going to be talking to? Maybe you haven't noticed, but it isn't exactly a metropolis here.'

'Excuse me,' said the tubby man.

'Excuse you? If Angela would have passed me the corkscrew it'd be halfway up your ... nose by now. And where did you get that mango?'

'What?'

'Jesus! That mango in your hand. Where did you get it?'

'In that grove thing, just over there.' He pointed energetically and the mango fell to the ground.

'There better be more,' said Peter.

They set off in the direction the man had pointed, into the darker, denser part of the forest.

'You got a name?' asked Angela.

'Me?' said the tubby man.

'Of course *you*,' said Peter.

'No.'

'What should we call him, Peter?' Angela asked.

'This guy,' said Peter, 'without a shadow of a doubt, is a Larry.'

* * *

Later, when the sky had turned a darker blue and some of the warmth had fallen from the air, Angela and Larry sat with their backs against trees, eating mangoes, while Peter tried to build a fire.

'You think we *need* a fire?' asked Angela. 'We've got blankets in our backpacks.'

'Who knows how cold it's going to get?' he said, balancing some twigs in a pyramid shape. 'Besides, what am I going to do for entertainment if I don't work out how to build a fire? Talk to you and Larry? I don't think so.'

'Why are you so *mean*, Peter? My God. Not everyone would know that you're joking.'

'What makes you think I'm joking? And how do you make this goddamn thing work?'

All the equipment in their packs had a sleek, polished design, making them appealing to look at and hold, but somewhat difficult to tell apart or actually use. Peter held the smooth cylindrical gadget that he suspected was for lighting fires, and clicked its button. Nothing happened, so he left it beside the pile of twigs and began another inspection of the contents of his rucksack.

Click.

'Hey Peter,' said Angela. 'Would you *look* what Larry did?'

Peter looked up and saw, with some annoyance, that Larry was holding the metal gadget in one hand and in the other a twig with a burning end. His half-eaten mango lay on the ground beside him.

'How d'you do that?' demanded Peter, snatching the gadget out of Larry's hand.

Angela said, 'Peter! Why you gotta be such a snatch-fingers?'

'I just operated it,' said Larry.

'A *snatch-fingers?*' said Peter. 'I'm just taking my lighter.'

'Which,' said Angela, 'he just showed you how to use.'

'Why can't he use his own?' said Peter.

Larry shrugged. 'Yours was lying there.'

'You got one though, don't you?' asked Peter.

'Yes.'

'What else you got?' Peter asked.

'Same as you, mostly.'

'What do you mean, *mostly*?'

'Mostly the same.'

'Jesus, what is wrong with this guy?'

'Peter!' scolded Angela.

'I'm gonna look through his backpack.'

Peter stood, snatched up Larry's rucksack from

where it rested against the trunk of a tree, and began to unzip it.

Angela stood too and grabbed hold of the rucksack from the other side.

'You get off his–' she began. But Peter had already pulled the zip open and snatched at something inside.

'He's got a saw!' shouted Peter.

He pulled it out of Larry's rucksack and brandished it triumphantly.

'You saw me struggling to collect wood. Why didn't you tell me you had a saw?'

Larry shrugged. 'You didn't ask.'

'What is *wrong* with this guy?' shouted Peter.

'Nothing,' said Angela. 'You just leave him alone.'

'But you got to admit, that's bad. He had a saw and he didn't tell me. And' – he spotted something else and pulled it from the bag – 'an axe! A goddamn axe! Jesus Christ, that's–'

'My God! Calm *down*, Peter. You didn't mean anything by it, did you, Larry?'

'Hi.'

It was a new voice, behind them.

They instantly fell silent and turned slowly around. The man who stood before them was young, tall and thin, with thick blond hair pushing out from under his hat and framing his tanned face. He had prominent blue eyes, a large nose and a child's jaw.

It was Angela who first found words.

'Wow. Yes. Hi. I'm Angela. This is Larry and this is Peter. Do you have a name?'

'I'm Fifi,' said the tall young man, and smiled a large white smile.

'You sure?' asked Peter. 'You remember your name?'

'Sure,' said Fifi, uncertainly.

'You got it written down anywhere? Any proof?'

'Probably, somewhere. Why wouldn't I be Fifi?'

Peter looked at his two companions' faces, saw that they weren't going to say anything, and went ahead. 'It's a dog's name.'

'What? Really?'

'Sure. Everyone knows. Right?'

Angela gave an apologetic smile, and Larry said, 'Yes.'

'You wake up this morning not knowing who or where you were?' asked Peter.

'Yes. But then the name Fifi just jumped into my mind. I really feel like that's my name.'

'You know what?' said Peter. 'Fine. You be Fifi. You can't be weirder than these two fruitcakes.'

'Ignore Peter,' said Angela. 'He's cranky.'

'And a snatch-fingers, Angela – don't forget to tell him that,' said Peter.

'Come on, Fifi,' said Angela. 'Sit down, why don't you? You want a mango?'

The next morning, strong sunlight poured through Peter's eyelids, warming his eyeballs and stirring his brain into waking. At first he again had no idea who or where he was, but then gradually the little he knew came back to him. He was Peter, and he was in a strange place, surrounded by trees, mangoes, coconuts and sleeping halfwits.

He walked a short distance away from their little clearing and dug himself a hole with Larry's axe. As he squatted over his little hole, he raised his eyes and saw again the mountain in the distance.

He wiped himself with a large leaf, decided against filling in the hole, and walked back to the clearing. There he packed up his things, taking the axe too, and set off for the mountain. He didn't wake the others. He couldn't bear to hear Angela's voice again, the way it always seemed to be simultaneously rising and trailing off. He couldn't face Larry or Fifi.

The forest grew first thicker and then more sparse. Stones appeared underfoot, and then there were outcrops of rock. A goat complained loudly and ran away, joining another in the distance. By the time the sun was high in the sky, he had reached the mountain. It was not the sort of mountain that required climbing; it was a mountain for walking and clambering up: an easy mountain. Nonetheless, his hat was damp with sweat by the time he arrived at the rocky peak, where the stone was speckled with a pinkish lichen. He sat down, took off the hat and looked around.

He could see now that he was indeed on an island, ringed with sandy beaches and surrounded by calm, sparkling blue sea. Behind him, back the way he had come, was forest. In front of him, on the other side of the mountain, the landscape diverged. Away to his left was a small lake, with brownish birds floating on it, and beyond it a low grassy hill beside the sea. Off to his right the land was more rocky, though still scattered with trees.

And then he saw them. At first he wasn't sure,

but he squinted his eyes and there was no doubt: more people. Five of them, three sitting in the shade of a large rock while another stood beneath a tree and the last paced about.

He sat for twenty minutes, then raised himself stiffly up and put on his hat. 'Goddamn it! For Chrissakes!' he said as he realised that his bald head had sunburned.

It took him at least as long to descend the other side of the mountain as it had to clamber up. He worried about tripping, about losing his footing and breaking a leg – and he didn't hold out much hope that Angela or Larry would think of coming to look for him.

When the ground levelled out again, he was just a few hundred feet from the group, but hidden from them by a large rock. He approached the rock, pressed his back to it and moved slowly around its surface, delaying the moment when he would appear to them. They were talking.

'Why not?' said one of them.

'Because someone will come and find us,' said another. 'We just need to stay right where we are.'

'And starve to death. That's crazy,' said the first person.

'No, what's crazy is marching off into the wilderness.'

'We already did that. I don't know why we didn't stay on the beach.'

'Sure, and dry our skins out so we shrivel up like walnuts,' said a third voice.

'Because there was no shelter on the beach and–'

'Right, and there's like *plenty* of shelter here?'

Peter stepped out.

'Hi,' he said.

There was a beat, then everyone started speaking at once.

'Oh my God!'

'Is this the rescue party? One guy?'

'Where are we?'

'Should we have waited on the beach?'

'Do you have any food?

'It is, like, so *good* to see someone new?'

Peter waved his arms to hush them.

'Calm down, folks,' said Peter. 'One at a time.'

'Are you here to rescue us?' asked a short, square-faced man with a deep tan and a barrel-like torso.

'Rescue you?' Peter's brain was working overtime.

'And do you have any food?' asked the square-faced barrel man.

'I got a little food. You like mango?'

'Oh my God! I *love* mango!' said the barrel man.

Peter removed his rucksack and took out the mango he had packed. The barrel man grabbed it and took a big bite.

'Hey, that's not all for you,' said one of the others – a slim man with straw-coloured hair.

The barrel man bent over the mango, using his shoulders and biceps as a wall between food and people.

'I got a little coconut milk as well,' said Peter. 'You want to try?'

He offered his canteen and the straw-haired man grabbed it and took a long drink.

'That mango was *so* good,' said the barrel man.

'You've finished it?' said the straw-haired man.

'Well you've finished his canteen,' said one of the others, a man with longish hair and a moustache.

'Where can we get more food?' asked a young woman with a tense voice, running her hands through her silky hair.

'Sit down,' said Peter, 'and I'll tell you what's going on.'

They sat obediently.

'First, let me introduce myself. I'm Peter. You got names?'

They looked at each other and then the barrel man wailed, 'We can't remember them!'

'You didn't make any up?' asked Peter.

They exchanged glances and shook their heads.

'Wait, I think I'm Tom,' said the straw-haired man. '*Tom.* That sounds like a name. Tom. *Tom.* Tom.' He tested the word out, obviously enjoying it. And there was something big and certain to the sound of it, in his accent.

'Fine, you be Tom,' said Peter. 'You did right to wait here. This is pretty much the only safe part of the island. And where I've just come from, the forest, is dangerous like you would not believe.'

'Dangerous how?'

'Wild animals, poisonous fish, the works. Unfortunately, that's where the food is. Luckily, when you been here a while like I have, you develop survival techniques. So, bottom line: yes, I can get you some food. But I need a little something to compensate me for the dangers.'

'What sort of little something?'

'What've you got in your backpacks?'

They unzipped them.

'There's some tools,' said Tom, 'but we're going to need those.'

'There's blankets,' said the barrel man.

'You all got blankets?' asked Peter.

They looked in their rucksacks and exchanged glances and yeses.

'Well give me those. You won't need them anyway – it's getting to the warm season.'

'Why do you want them?' asked Tom.

'I like blankets. Something wrong with that?'

2

MISS KAMI

There was soft, cool cotton beneath her cheek and fingertips, and a light silken quilt was pulled up to her nose. Her heart was beating fast from her dream – a dream of darkness and light, of being pulled down, drowning – but that was already dropping away, receding into the shadows of her mind. She had been for a long swim the evening before and could still feel the heaviness in her limbs. They felt clumsy as she stirred, uncurled herself, and turned onto her back. Only then did Mariko open her eyes.

The sun glowed through paper blinds, touching every part of the white room in which she slept. The walls were coated in a material that made the soft, white sunlight seem to shine from inside them. She sat up and reached for the white kimono that lay neatly folded beside her futon. As she put it on, she saw and was pleased by the delicate floral pattern inside it, hand-stitched in the lightest possible grey. Then she sat cross-legged on her futon and reached out for a cup as fine and pale as an eggshell, into which a silver machine had just poured the only black thing in the room: coffee.

Her heart had slowed a little, but she could still feel its irregular beat against her ribs. The coffee would not help that, but it might fool her into thinking there was some reason for it other than anxiety about her meeting later that morning. She took the cup in both hands, protected from its heat by the cuffs of her kimono. She looked into the black pool, raised it ceremoniously to her lips, and drank. It was hot, strong, bitter and deep, warming a spark at the centre of her mind. She sipped it down greedily, like a cat at a puddle, and followed it with an orange and a few mouthfuls of sweet breakfast rice.

In the white bathroom, she showered in a pod that sent hard jets of water at her from every angle. After this liquid massage, the water faded away and warm air was blown in, gently drying her. She stepped out, put on a loose shirt and trousers in lemon yellow, then went to her meditation chamber, which was saffron and red. White was for sleep, for rest. Meditation was an energetic calmness, and she entered the right state most easily when she was surrounded with colour.

She sat cross-legged again, eyes lightly closed, head down, hands open and resting on her knees. All her attention was on her breathing and the energy that flowed through her body. She felt her heartbeat slow down, steady itself. Calm came for a few seconds, perhaps minutes, and then left her again. She glimpsed, just behind every thought, the idea of the meeting that morning with Mr Ellory. Her heartbeat speeded up again, its rhythm jagged.

She stood and went to her workspace, took a large sheet of clean paper and began, in ink, a mandala. She worked without thinking, instinctively laying out and elaborating the circular pattern that came from her brush. But then her heart gave another thud. She fumbled a stroke, smudged a spoke of the mandala. And it was ruined.

An hour later, she stepped out of the black Elcor limousine, wearing dark glasses in bamboo frames with a white knee-length coat. Mr Mori, waiting at the curb, greeted her with a bow and closed the car door behind her.

'Miss Kami, it is a pleasure to see you again. Thank you so much for visiting us today.' His smile was full, square, precise.

'Good morning, Mr Mori.'

He held out his hand, indicating the lobby of the company's headquarters, then followed slightly behind her. He did not touch her, no doubt knowing she would find it intolerable. But she could feel his hand an inch away from her back, between her shoulder-blades, a protective or propelling gesture, and this too was unbearable.

The ceiling of the lobby soared far overhead. The space was divided by four huge steel pillars. The floor was black stone and the walls Elcor's deep blue. Above the long reception desk, the company's name was stencilled in silver letters six feet high. Mariko and Mr Mori walked briskly through security gates held open by two men in suits of Elcor blue, and then took a waiting elevator to the top floor.

In the boardroom, one massive wall was a

darkened aquarium, filled with small fish glowing white, so it seemed that galaxies of stars were endlessly coalescing and dispersing. The wall opposite was made of glass, and through it Mariko could see southwest across New York, over the bottom of Central Park and down to the harbour. Running nearly the whole length of the room, between the star aquarium and the living mural of New York, was a polished table made from a slice of a single Redwood tree. At the far end sat a white-haired man, built to the same outsized scale as the room, solid like a toad, with tanned and burnished skin that shone like the Redwood: Mr Ellory. He sat deep in a high-backed black leather chair, holding an unlit cigar in his hand.

At Mr Ellory's right hand sat a man in his early thirties, with a thin face, long nose and dark-golden hair pulled back in a sleek ponytail. He wore a well-cut black suit with a white shirt and no tie. When Mariko neared the head of the table, the younger man rose and held out a hand. She acknowledged it with a slight bow, but did not touch him.

Mr Mori smiled his precise, square smile and held the chair, gesturing Mariko to sit. She did so, relaxing a little as he removed his hands from the back of her chair and then sat a respectful distance away. She kept her eyes on her bamboo-framed sunglasses, which she held in her lap.

'Kami San,' said Ellory, addressing her. His voice was deep and rough, echoing in his chest, as though he had consumed a hundred thousand cigars and still had room for more. He spoke slowly, in a faded Texan accent, exhaling his words like smoke. And he moved very little, as if he were mid-nap and didn't like to wake himself. 'Should we be concerned?'

She nodded.

'It's hard?' he asked. 'Keeping up with what's happening on the island?'

She was silent a long time, perhaps a minute, before she said, 'For me, the island is very upsetting. I do not watch or listen these last days.'

'Could it be two weeks?' asked Ellory's voice. She still did not raise her eyes, but she nodded.

'Perhaps, yes. When they got to the island, for the first week, I watch, I hope. Then for three more weeks I watch and listen, but I do not wish to watch or listen. Then for two weeks I can not watch or listen any more. It is upsetting.'

'And could it be, Kami San, that I am also upset?'

She nodded.

'And do you think that our customers might be upset?' asked Ellory. 'When they come back home and their memories are restored. Could they be upset that they did not get what was promised them?'

Again, she nodded.

The man with the sleek ponytail gave a polite, deliberate cough, and the older man said, 'Have I introduced Joshua McVeigh? He's our new head of Luxury Sales. Perhaps he might have an interesting perspective on this?'

Mariko nodded at McVeigh, who smoothed the front of his white shirt and smiled.

'Miss Kami,' said McVeigh, 'I have heard so much about you, and let me tell you that it is an honour to finally get to meet you – you are my favourite contemporary multidisciplinary artist. Check that: my favourite artist. Period. Can I just say, I loved *Monolith*. Powerful work. But I've only been with Elcor three weeks, and until yesterday I was spending *all* my time – and I mean *all my time* – on troubleshooting our joint venture with Louis Vuitton. Let me tell you' – he seemed about to head off on a tangent, but caught Ellory's eye and wheeled himself back – 'about that some other time. So, I'm new around here and I would love for you to fill me in a little on this project. Would that be possible?'

Mariko closed her eyes and took a deep breath, but it was Mr Mori who spoke.

'Miss Kami spotted a market,' he said, pausing to refresh his smile for McVeigh, 'and a high-value way of exploiting it.'

Mariko's eyes snapped open, though she kept her gaze on her lap.

'I made an observation,' she corrected. Her voice was soft and slow, sing-song, and she emphasised every third or fourth word – for rhythm, not meaning. 'I observe that there are many people here in the United States who are very rich, but who are alienated from everything that can bring true satisfaction: companionship, co-operation, work with hands. Yes – the things that keep us in this moment, truly tasting the world. I believe our spirits choose to come to this world. We came to experience love, to learn about love. But we forget this is why we came. I observe that there are many people here who do not experience real love, and who suffer for it, despite all their money.'

'Being rich sucks, right?' Joshua McVeigh

laughed, but the other two men didn't join in, so he quickly faded his laughter down to a concerned chuckle – as though he too had long been troubled by this issue. Then he looked earnestly at each of them in turn and said, 'Excuse me.'

'I began to think,' said Mariko. 'I think these alienated people will benefit much from experiencing the togetherness that poverty can bring. I travelled in Vietnam. I saw there that many poor people are much happier than the rich. And I think to myself that this is because the poor live lives that force them to pay attention to the physical world around them, and to the people around them. They live a communal life, surrounded by other people. In these conditions bonds of love form. Strong, natural.'

'So, to be clear, and I don't wish to sound blunt: you get rich guys to pay to live in a slum?' asked McVeigh.

'My first idea is to take these people to live in a slum. Yes. But Mr Mori points out the disadvantages. Slums are full of love. Yes. But there are many diseases and dangers. Many things that rich Westerners will not cope with. And these will distract them too much. They will also be outsiders. And so they will not have the true benefits of being slum-dwellers.'

'Yah,' said McVeigh. 'And I would not like to manage those security risks. Can you imagine what happens when the slum guys find out who their visitors are? Can you say "kidnapping"? Do I hear the word "ransom"?' He smiled and seemed on the verge of laughing again, but saw their expressions and stopped himself.

Ellory nodded and Mariko continued. 'But I think to myself. Why is there happiness in slums? How can I create these conditions without having also the dangers?'

'I am intrigued to discover the answer, Miss Kami,' said McVeigh. 'Intrigued.'

'Life must not be too easy. But it must not be too hard. Food, for example. It must be scarce enough that every time one eats, it is a pleasure. But it must not be so scarce that one feels the suffering of starvation, or the anxiety that one does not have enough food to live. A little hunger sharpens the senses. But too much makes one desperate. And work. There must be simple, physical work. And the reward is food and shelter: simple pleasures. Above all, there must be the conditions for togetherness. People must find each other, co-operate. All should be equal from the very beginning, but each should have something – some little tool perhaps, that is unique to them. When everyone has something to contribute, there is co-operation.'

'Okay. So, I am getting a real clear picture of the thinking behind this. But I'm thinking, commercially, what's the offer here? What's the package?'

Mariko looked blankly at him.

'May I?' asked Mr Mori, offering his precise smile again, glancing from Mariko to Ellory. They nodded. 'The package, Mr McVeigh, was this. We looked for an uninhabited island with a pleasant tropical climate and an adequate supply of naturally occurring food. That was the core of the commercial proposition. We've mentioned the commercial challenges involved in selling holidays in a slum to high net-worth individuals. But a chance to start over on a paradise island? A chance to find out how people react to the real you, not distracted by your wealth? The chance to discover real life: community, love, beaches? Well, that is a significantly easier sales proposition.'

'Thank you,' said McVeigh, 'for that perfect summary, Mr Mori. Now a few minutes ago, Mr

Ellory, you mentioned something about our customers' memories being restored? Can I dig a little deeper there?'

Mr Ellory turned his head slowly towards Mariko.

She said, 'It is essential for people to leave behind their old identities. That means their memories. I would not compromise on this. Without this temporary amnesia, people will judge each other – and themselves – by their wealth, by their life history, by what they have achieved or have not achieved. But this judging is the very thing that has made them unhappy. So, we make them forget who they were. And for the first time, they are simply a person. A person among other people.'

Mr Mori said, 'And this proved a very astute move. In fact, it turned out to be a key selling point: "Take a holiday from yourself." That was the line, and it was strong, sales-wise. A product like this, especially in its first generation, you don't want to go for billboards, TV adverts. It has to be subtle. You get the word out to personal shoppers, elite therapists, lifestyle consultants. But that line, that was our pitch, and that played strongly.'

'So this memory loss, how was it delivered?' asked McVeigh.

'We consulted widely,' said Mr Mori, 'and I'm confident that what we developed is state of the art. It commences with a two-day induction period, consisting of hypnotic suggestions, combined with short-term memory suppressants and relaxants – mild tranquillisers. This forms what we call an "air lock" – a period between the old life and the new, in which no new memories are laid down. There is thus no perceived continuity between the two. At the end of this air-lock period, a stronger tranquilliser is administered. This takes the customer out for about eight hours. During that time, we get every customer to their start positions on the island. They all begin alone, but no more than five minutes' walk from another person. When they awake the post-hypnotic suggestions kick in: they feel deeply relaxed and have no memory of who they are or of their previous life. To be exact, they have basically no episodic memories from their lives, but they remember categories and words. They'd recognise a banana, for example, but wouldn't know whether they'd ever eaten one. The amnesia affects different people in slightly different ways, but that's the broad brush.'

'And this amnesia has held?'

'Yes. No memories have returned. We did have … cause for mild alarm early on when one of our customers – Fifi Maddox, son of the rock star Brian Maddox – called himself by his real name. But that seems to be an anomaly, perhaps a coincidence.'

'So there's no danger that the amnesia will wear off?'

'None,' said Mr Mori. 'We tested it on interns. It's good for at least six months. Of course, we can terminate it early if we wish. And we build in "reintegration cues" to the hypnotic suggestions, so that when the customers return they can remember both their time on the island and their previous life, enabling them to integrate the two in a trauma-free fashion. Our interns said that it was the greatest experience of their life: a way to find out who they really are, without irrelevances such as how they did in school, which fraternity accepted them at college, and so on.'

'Our interns think those things are irrelevant?' asked McVeigh, frowning.

'Professionally, highly relevant. But spirit-wise,

they consider those are not the main plays. Now, does that bring you up to speed, Josh?'

McVeigh nodded. 'Uh-huh. Just two things. How long have these guys been on the island now? And what monitoring systems do we have in place? Do we have any feet on the ground?'

'In answer to your first question: they've been there six weeks now, out of a contracted twelve-week stay. On monitoring: we have no people on the ground. It was felt' – Mr Mori shot a glance at Mariko – 'that this would negatively impact the experience. However, we have advanced satellite monitoring, producing video feeds in near real time. And we have glider drones and water-borne systems for picking up audio. It's fragmentary, but we can usually get the gist of what's going on.'

'So what is going on?' asked McVeigh. He looked at each of the other three, his eyes coming to rest on Mariko, who looked at the floor. She could not bear to answer, or even to think about the answer.

Mori stepped in. 'There is a … uh … lack of bonding occurring. The focus is not on the optimal thematic area.'

'Can you say more?' asked McVeigh.

Mori glanced at Mariko, then said, 'By this

stage, we had projected we would see participants taking long walks together along the beautiful beaches, getting together to play games or engage in leisurely foraging for the abundant food. We were thinking campfires in the evening, shared laughter …' He trailed off.

'And they're not doing those things?'

'Far from it,' said Mori.

Ellory did not turn his head more than two inches, but it was as though a spotlight had been turned on McVeigh. 'Suggestions?' he prompted.

'Excuse me,' said McVeigh, 'but I'm kind of direct in my approach to problem-solving. What's top of mind for me is this: just send Miss Kami in by helicopter. She can land, tour the island in a jeep and deliver a top-line presentation explaining to people how they should behave, in regard to mutual bonding. I'm thinking–'

He stopped abruptly as Mariko lifted her gaze from her lap and stared straight into his eyes.

'If,' she said, 'it is as simple as saying "you bond now" then there is no need for the island. These people must learn how to love one another. That is what they need: to learn. If I appear and tell them, that is completely against the point.'

Mori added, 'This may be a side point, but I

would worry that seeing a well-known figure such as Miss Kami in a helicopter could potentially weaken the induced amnesia.'

'Yet,' said Ellory, allowing the word to hang for a second or two in the air, 'doesn't something need to happen? Can we let it go on like it is?' He often spoke in questions, but his questions were commands.

McVeigh stroked his chin, with its short, manicured beard. 'Well, I see that solution was perhaps a little *too* direct, and I acknowledge your reservations. But these individuals, somewhere inside of them, they must know why they purchased this product. Can we remind them of that in a more subtle way? Is there any scope for broadcasting subliminal messages – so that these customers will be influenced without realising it?'

Mori shook his head. 'We have no public-address facilities on the island.'

'To learn, they must make a choice,' said Mariko.

'Then … okay, how about this. We send someone who seems just like everyone else – dressed the same, same equipment. This guy's our messenger. He says he has no idea where the message comes from, only that he believes it. And he tells them – gently, subtly – "Behave optimally". We can refine the message, but you get my drift. And then he role-models the appropriate bonding behaviour. That way we're giving them a reminder, but there's no helicopter, no famous artist – they're still in the world and they get to choose. And the more of them choose right, the more it impacts the others and encourages them to choose right. It might not work for everyone, but we could potentially significantly impact the numbers who may not be satisfied when the experience is over. And I mean impact those numbers by a downward vector.'

Ellory nodded: a single motion of his monolithic head.

Mori turned to Mariko and smiled, waiting for her reaction.

'This messenger,' she said, 'how would he be chosen?'

Mori said, 'Miss Kami is right. The messenger is key.'

McVeigh leaned back in his chair. 'I have a candidate in mind. I use him in deals where tact and diplomacy are of the essence. Nice guy, family man, very charming, a hard worker, and smart –

Harvard MBA. He … let me see if I can get him in here. Excuse me for one minute.'

He pulled a phone from his pocket and pressed a couple of buttons.

'Hi Amy. Is Brad available right now? … Okay, what time does he get out of the meeting?'

Mr Ellory held out his hand to McVeigh, who said, 'One second, Amy' and passed the phone into his boss's palm.

Ellory pressed the red cancel button, ending the call, his thumb almost covering the phone's screen. He passed the phone back to McVeigh.

'You're going, Josh. Yourself.'

'Me?' said McVeigh. 'Absolutely. I mean, absolutely. It's just, I'm still new to my role here, excited to be learning about it, I've got back-to-back lunches lined up, and the guy I was thinking of …'

'We managed without you before you arrived. We can manage without you again, for a little while.'

Mr Mori said, 'You know, Josh, when you were describing your candidate, I thought, "That guy sounds just like Josh." And I can't believe we have another executive with superior tact and delicacy in dealing with high net-worth individuals than you.'

McVeigh held up his hands and smiled helplessly.

'Is this not important?' said Ellory. 'Can Elcor afford to fail in this?'

'Sure,' said McVeigh. 'I'll go. I won't let you down, Mr Ellory.'

3

THE COMING OF KEITH

'Hey, could I get a cup of coffee in here?'

Peter shouted this without looking up from the ledger that lay before him on his desk. When there was no immediate answer he sighed deeply, put down his pen and straightened his back, the better to shout again.

'Hey! Are you deaf? Has that goddamn hair of yours worked its way into your ears?'

The stairs creaked, and then there was the sound of footsteps hastily climbing. He leaned back in his chair and put his hands over his face.

'Every goddamn idiot here is trying to drive me crazy,' he said to himself.

The door opened and Angela walked into the wooden room.

'Angela,' he said. 'We were just talking about you.'

Angela looked around in alarm. 'But you're on your own, Peter. There's no one here.'

'I was talking to the wall, Angela. It has the best line in conversation on this goddamn island.'

Angela dithered for a couple of seconds, visibly unsure whether to put the half coconut shell of steaming black liquid on the desk or hand it to Peter.

'Where does it always go, Angela?'

'We've only had coffee for a couple of weeks …'

'Right. And in that time where have I always told you to put it?'

'The desk?'

'That's right, Angela. So put it on the desk.'

She put the coffee down carefully on the edge of Peter's huge, gleaming desk, which had taken a large part of a tree to make.

'Jesus, if I can invent coffee, you should at least be able to put it down in the right place.'

'But it was Larry who …'

'Hey! Enough of that. Sure, Larry tried grinding and roasting coconut and then dripping boiling water through it. But it was me who saw the potential. I funded him and I named it.'

'I'm sorry, Peter.'

'Jesus, Angela. Could you act like you *want* to keep your job?'

'I don't want a job, Peter. I want things to be the way they were. I want to sit on the beach and eat mangoes.'

'Sure, let's all go sit on the beach and eat mangoes, see how quickly we go broke.'

She looked at him with wide eyes, just for a moment, and then hurried out of the room.

Peter stood up and kicked his chair over, swore, sighed, and walked over to the window that faced southwest – the best view. His office was on the second floor, making it the second-highest point in town. From this window he could see the forest, already a quarter cleared, and in front of it the newly planted mango groves. Closer in, clustered near to his own building, were shacks built to a standard pattern, where the middle-class people lived – Angela, for the moment, still among them. A little distance from them – huddled around the goose farm and industrial sites – were the tarpaulins, lean-tos and temporary shelters for the sweat-workers. A small group of people were just leaving them, walking to their shift at the fish-processing shack, where the fishermen brought what they had caught in their Larries – trawler nets made from creepers, which Peter had graciously named after their inventor.

Peter had economic interests in every building and trade he could see from this window. They said there wasn't a foot of forest cleared, a house built or a fish gutted from which Peter didn't earn a coconut or two.

He turned away, picked up his coffee from his desk and moved over to the east window – the window he usually avoided. There was bad news through the east window, but sometimes he couldn't help looking. He took a gulp of coffee and winced. His headache was awful: a sort of generalised pounding with irregular flashes behind the eyes. The door opened behind him, the sound making him jump. But it was only Angela, carrying a wooden plate on which lay four mango cookies, carefully arranged.

She saw him looking out of the window.

'Is that why you're so *antsy* today, Peter? Because of *Tom*? Why do you *let* him get to you?'

'I don't let him get to me, Angela. I just notice that he has the only three-floor building on this island. How's that supposed to make me feel, when I've only got two? Great? Successful?'

'But you *are* successful. I mean, when I see the *ledger* …'

'What you should see when you check the ledger is that I missed my income target for this month. You know I was going for a one-half increase. What do I get instead? An increase of 45 hundred-parts.'

'But that's *nearly* a one-half increase, Peter.'

'Nearly isn't enough, Angela. Nearly is failure. Nearly means I probably don't have enough to pay the wood-workers to build an extra floor on my house. And that means my house carries on telling everyone that Tom is winning.'

'But you have your *strong-room*, Peter. Tom's is *nowhere near* as good. And you probably *are* still the richest guy on the whole island. Or *at least* a very close second …'

Peter flinched. 'Take the cookies away, Angela. I don't want them.'

'Peter …' she said.

'You heard me. I said take them away, Angela.'

He stared fixedly out of the window as Angela picked up the plate and left the room. The door closed and her footsteps slowly descended the stairs.

Tom's secretary was Susan – beautiful and

efficient Susan, with her silky hair and her alluring tenseness. But there was no way Peter could compete with the package Tom was laying on for her – a hundred coconuts a week, he'd heard, plus accommodation and blanket rental.

That was one consolation. Securing ownership of nine-tenths of the islanders' blankets in that first week had been a smart move. As well as setting up a continuing source of revenue for Peter, it had laid the basis for the island's wage economy, since people had been obliged to work so that they could earn enough to rent their blankets back once the nights turned chilly.

But even there, Tom had bested him, managing to acquire at least three-quarters of the stoves in various deals. In the end, that was a stronger monopoly: there were already experiments in weaving goats' hair, meaning people would soon be able to buy new blankets, whereas large-scale metal production was at least a year away, even with the enhanced research budget that Peter's latest plan envisioned.

He took another sip of coffee. Laughter rose from among the shacks, in the area around the workshop that turned the wood-pulp into paper for his ledgers and filtered the octopus ink for his precision-cut goose-feather pen. Peter knew that if he could just overtake Tom, the headache would disappear and he'd be happy. He imagined himself one floor higher – no, two floors higher – with Susan sitting at a smaller desk in the same room. 'What would you like me to do today, Peter?' she would ask, and then she would re-cross her legs and tensely stroke her silky hair. Yes, one day he'd have enough to be happy. He could just lie on the beach all day and stare at the sky, maybe take a walk in the Forest Preservation Zone.

But daydreaming wouldn't get him anywhere. He tore his eyes away from the view of Tom's three-floor house and stamped back to his desk. He needed to know the figures inside out before his meeting with the wood-workers.

An hour later, Peter walked downstairs. Outside the strongroom door sat Barrel, Peter's security man.

Barrel stood as Peter approached, and raised his eyebrows half an inch – it was his own form of greeting, as well as being almost the full extent of his facial mobility.

'Okay, let's open her up,' said Peter.

Barrel nodded and picked up a piece of shaped wood. The strongroom was built on to one side of the ground-floor room, with double-thickness walls and no windows. The only way in was through a door inside Peter's house, and that door was fitted with the island's only lock. Peter and Barrel each had a large wooden key, which they simultaneously inserted into holes on either side of the door. When they turned their keys, there was a creaking of wood as Larry's mechanism lifted up the stout piece of timber that barred the door on the inside.

Barrel opened the door and shone his wind-up torch into the dark. There, stacked in crates on the shelves, were more coconuts than anyone had seen together in one place – at least since the first week on the island, when coconuts had lain abundantly on the ground. Peter picked up his ledger and walked in.

'What's the tally, Barrel?'

'My tally says we've got four thousand, one hundred seventy-eight.'

'What?'

'Ah, four one seven eight?'

'The ledger says four two one four.'

'I ... Well, ah, what can I tell you, Peter?'

'I don't know, maybe you can tell me where thirty-six coconuts have gone. Let me see the tally sheet.'

Barrel took a sheaf of papers that hung from a hook on the wall and passed them to Peter.

'What is this mess? Can't you keep a simple tally?'

'I try really hard.'

'Yeah, well. Maybe you don't want to keep it too accurate.'

'What are you saying, Peter?'

'What do you think I'm saying?'

'You think I took them?'

'Did I say that?'

'No, but–'

'So why're you talking about stealing my coconuts? You got a guilty conscience?'

Barrel looked at the ground and said nothing.

'This place needs a proper inventory,' said Peter. 'When coconuts go missing and you go talking about stealing, my nasty suspicious mind gets to wondering. But we don't have time for this now. We've got to meet these builders by halfway post-noon and they're on the other side of town.'

They closed up the strongroom and set off for

their meeting, Barrel hanging back and looking – so far as his static features would allow it – unhappy.

'Ah, come on,' said Peter. 'Forget it – till the inventory. You wanna go by the beach?'

Barrel nodded slightly, and Peter thought he saw a hint of a smile.

'Okay then. Let's go by the beach, take a nice walk along the seafront.'

They turned right and walked past a row of standard middle-class shacks, past the paper factory and the furniture workshop, and down to the end of the street, where it met the beach. Peter stopped and stared.

'You see this?' said Peter, pointing to Luke's house, which stood on the corner at the end of the street. 'Would you call this a two-floor house?'

'Not at all. It's just a one-floor with a … a kind of shack thing on top.'

'How come I never noticed this before? Luke, you lousy bastard, you're trying to make out that you've got a two-floor house! Like that slob could ever afford a two-floor house! You make paper, you schmuck, you can't afford a two-floor! So he puts a few bits of wood up there. I bet he calls it a balcony or a sun-terrace or some bullshit like that!'

'Sun terrace sounds classy,' said Barrel.

Peter looked at him. 'I gotta get a third floor.'

'You'll get one.'

'Well, I better not miss out on a deal by thirty-six coconuts, that's all I …' He stopped. 'Hey, look at that.' He looked up again at Luke's house. 'He's got his sun terrace facing the wrong way, so he can't see out to sea. What's the poi–'

But he noticed Barrel had stopped listening and was looking along the beach.

Peter followed the direction of Barrel's gaze. Midway up the beach, a crowd of people had clustered around something on the ground.

'What's going on over there?' asked Barrel.

'I don't know, but I hope nobody's planning on getting paid for it.'

They padded across the soft sand towards the group. The people on the edges were standing on tiptoe to see over the heads of those in the centre, who were kneeling, focusing intently on something.

'What are they looking at?' asked Barrel.

'Those numbskulls? Probably just an interestingly shaped rock.'

Someone on the outskirts of the group turned to them. It was Andrew, the fisherman.

'There's a new guy!' he said.

Fifi, who was standing beside Andrew, also turned. 'They say he walked out of the ocean!'

'No kidding?' said Peter.

'We looked out and there he was, up to his waist in the water, just wading on in …' said Andrew.

'With this smile on his face,' added Fifi.

'He has a message for us,' said Andrew.

'Well,' said Peter, 'maybe I got a message for him.'

People must have heard Peter's voice, because they began to shift, opening up the circle. At the centre, surrounded by kneeling people, sat a man Peter had never seen before. He had long hair that clung wetly to the sides of his thin face. On the top of his head, where the hair was beginning to dry, a few golden-brown strands reached upwards. A short beard dripped from his chin, and he was dressed exactly as they had all been when they arrived – an olive-green jacket and blue trousers. Beside him sat a rucksack, dark with water. And in his hands he held a sock, which he was wringing out. His feet were bare.

'… I mean, hello, do I hear the word "regret?"'

he was saying excitedly to someone who crouched beside him. 'Excuse me, I'm a very direct person …'

And then he noticed the gap that had opened and he looked up and met Peter's eye.

'Hi,' said Peter. 'I'm Peter.'

'Hi,' said the man. 'Good to meet you, Peter.'

It seemed to Peter, in the instant their eyes met, that the man recognised him. But then the man smiled and the moment passed.

'So, they say you came in from the ocean,' said Peter, and the crowd made the sound that a group of people make when they agree wordlessly.

'I don't remember. First thing I knew I was sitting on this beach.'

'Just like the rest of us!' someone else said.

'Exactly,' said Peter. 'This is normal. This is the way it is. We arrive on the beach, we don't know anything. But you get a name, you work hard and pretty soon you're pulling down a decent number of coconuts every week, renting a decent shack.'

Someone said, 'Peter hasn't heard the message.'

The man with the thin face and the long, wet hair said, 'Yah, I have a message.'

'You've what now?' said Peter.

'I have a message. When I woke up, the only

thing I knew is that I'd been sent with a message for all of you. It–'

'A message from who?'

'I don't know. I don't think that's material at this point. The key point here is that you've deviated from the optimal course, and I believe you'll be disappointed with yourselves. You've gotten fixated on ownership, on material wealth and status.'

'Wait a minute,' said Peter. 'We're proud of what we got. We arrived here with squat, and now look at us. Okay, some of us work a little harder than others and have a little more to show for it ...'

'But honestly, excuse me for being direct, but this is ridiculous,' said the man. 'I mean, what you've got here is nothing compared with what you have back in the United State–'

He stopped, as though he had said too much.

'The United State?' said Peter.

'Forget that. Excuse me – I misspoke.' The man scowled, as though annoyed with himself. 'I'm trying to say that you came here to ... experience love. That's what you need to focus on. From day one you had enough to eat, enough shelter, enough to keep yourselves healthy. Love is what you need to focus on. It's where you need to channel your energy.'

There was a general murmur of approval from the crowd.

'Right,' said Peter. 'Sure. And we believe you because everybody knows the wettest guy is always the smartest.'

'This is not about being smart, Peter,' said the man, who had started to put his socks back on. 'Just listen to the message. You know it's right, deep down. Listen to how it feels. And forget me – forget whether I'm wet or dry or dumb or smart – I'm just the messenger.'

'Well you did a bang-up job. I'll be sure to tell – oh wait, you don't *know* who sent this bullshit message.'

'Hey!' said a voice in the crowd, reprovingly. 'Don't pick on him!'

'Yeah,' someone else agreed. 'Be nice.'

'Who said that?' said Peter, furious. Silence returned.

The man stopped putting his socks on and looked up at Peter. Their eyes met and neither looked away.

'This is not bullshit,' said the man. 'Just think

about it a while, just feel whether it's right. That's all I ask.'

'Do you have any proof of what you've said?'

The man smiled wryly and shook his head. 'Only the message itself. That's my proof.'

'But he's here,' said someone else. 'Surely that's our proof.'

'We're all here, goddamn it,' said Peter. 'We all appeared. That's just what happens. It doesn't mean that any old bullshit that falls out of your mouth is the truth. He's probably delirious.'

'What's delirious?' someone in the crowd asked.

'I don't know,' shouted Peter. 'It's just a thing.'

'Hey,' said Andrew. 'Maybe that's the proof. Where do all these words we don't know come from? Why do we have ideas about things we've never seen? It all comes from somewhere – from the same place as the message maybe.'

'Right,' said Peter. 'That place being my ass. Do you ever listen to yourself? Where do bullshit words come from? From our imagination.'

'But where does our imagination come from?' asked Andrew, with the air of someone making a devastatingly clever point.

'WHO GIVES A SHIT?' roared Peter.

'Hey, do you know where we came from?' someone asked the new arrival.

'I can't tell you,' said the man with the dripping golden hair.

'He already said: from the United State,' said Andrew.

'Why don't we remember who we are when we arrive? Why don't we remember the United State?' asked Caroline, who worked in the ink factory.

'Because it's a piece of manifest bullshit,' said Peter, butting in.

'*He* remembers, you can tell. He just doesn't want to tell us. What's your name?'

'I have no name,' said the man. 'And it doesn't matter where we come from, only how we are now, with each other. When all this ends, you won't care about coconuts and possessions. You'll see that the whole point of it is love.'

Everyone was silent a while. Peter looked down at the man, who was smiling slightly, his sock still clutched in his hand.

'So possessions aren't important?' said Peter.

'No,' said the man.

'Then,' said Peter, 'you won't mind if I take your backpack.'

The man looked up at him and met his eyes

again. There was total silence. No one around them moved. Even breathing seemed to have stopped. Peter felt that if the silence lasted another second, he would punch the man right through his damp beard and utterly destroy him.

'Sure,' said the man, smiling again. 'Go ahead.'

Someone in the crowd groaned, as though they were all losing something.

The man reached behind him and picked up the wet rucksack, holding it out to Peter. Peter took it, holding it by the handle on top to avoid getting himself wet.

'Thanks,' said Peter. 'Let me give you something in return. A name.'

'Okay.'

'You can be … Keith.'

'Keith?'

'Yeah, Keith.'

Then Peter turned and walked away. Barrel fell in beside him, and they went on to their meeting with the builders. It was already halfway post-noon.

4

PICNIC ON THE MOUNT

The crowd had melted away, back to their jobs. And Josh McVeigh, who was now called Keith, sat there alone on the beach, his clothes still damp, staring out at the sea.

Josh who was called Keith regretted accepting this assignment, regretted giving his backpack away, regretted delivering the message the moment he'd arrived. He had been overconfident. He could see that now. A message like this needed focus-grouping, refining, tailoring to its audience. And then a comms plan should be carefully constructed, the delivery mechanisms selected with care. After all, this was still – in the end – all about selling a niche product at a significant mark-up to high-net-worth individuals.

'You Keith?' It was a voice behind him, making him jump.

Keith turned.

'Hi, I'm Ben.' The man was standing a few feet away. He was heavy-set, with dark skin, longish hair and a moustache.

'Hey Ben,' said Keith, getting to his feet and holding out his hand. 'Great to meet you.'

'Heard you might need a job,' said Ben, shaking it.

Keith thought about this. It actually couldn't hurt. They really had made a tactical error in concentrating exclusively on top-level messaging and neglecting practicalities. He had no idea how he was going to eat or where he would sleep.

'I'm currently in the job market, yes,' said Keith, adding instinctively, 'I'm weighing up a number of different options and opportunities right now.'

'Well I own the lumberyard. We're pretty busy at the moment – Peter just ordered a new floor for his house. Could do with an extra pair of hands.'

'Great. Timber is a very interesting space right now. I'd be excited to get in on the ground floor.'

Ben looked slightly puzzled, but smiled. 'Heard you, uh, lost your backpack.'

Keith laughed to cover his annoyance at this mistake. 'Yes. That was … careless of me.'

'Listen, I'm not making the big coconuts around here, so I can't offer you much. But you could sleep in the lumberyard – just till you get on your feet. Meals included. And I'll rent a blanket for you.'

Keith was about to begin negotiating, but then he remembered the second part of his mission: modelling the correct behaviour.

'Great package,' he said. 'Yah, I think that pretty much covers the essential elements I'm looking for.'

'Sorry, I can only offer you three coconuts a week, though.'

Keith laughed again, this time genuinely.

'What's funny?' asked Ben. 'Okay, I could probably go to four. I mean, you look strong.'

Keith looked down at his body. Of course he looked strong. He worked in the high-net-worth sector, where a tan, twelve percent body fat and defined abs were as essential as a well-cut suit. *Wealth respects health*, his first boss used to say.

'Five then,' said Ben, 'but then I'm really having to make economies elsewhere.'

'I have to level with you,' said Keith. 'Excuse me,

but I'm a very direct person. I am not incentivised by coconuts. I don't need them. What motivates me is just the basics: food, shelter, a blanket, good people around me, and knowing I've done a solid day's work.'

'Really?' said Ben.

'Sure. Coconuts are just …' Keith trailed off, searching for something to compare them to which was more obviously unnecessary. Then, on a sudden inspiration, he said, 'They're what people collect instead of love.'

'Okay,' said Ben, uncertainly. 'I'll set aside three a week for you though, because I really think you're going to need them. You'll want to start saving for a down payment on a shack at some point.'

They set off together for the lumberyard.

After a while, Ben said, 'I heard about what you said – about the United State. You believe that? That's where we get our reward?'

'I may have misspoken earlier – I was a little lightheaded from the swim ashore. What I actually meant to say was that we all need to work together to achieve a united state right here on the island, and that the optimal way to achieve that would be this recognition that we came here, fundamentally, to experience love. That's the message I'm bringing. Does that resonate at all?'

'You didn't talk about the great riches waiting for us in the United State? Because that's what Fifi said.'

How could he have been so careless? It was because he had neglected his swimming since his daughter had arrived. That short swim – in clothes and backpack – from the boat to the beach had meant he'd arrived just not quite sharp enough.

'I was speaking metaphorically,' he said. 'The United State is actually more of an internal thing. It's in your heart. And the way to achieve it is by focusing on the here and now, and by behaving in a selfless fashion towards others. That's really the top-line message here.'

That *was* the top-line message. And he was pretty sure his bonus depended on his ability to persuade everyone that it was the truth.

There was a glowing, comforting field of orange-red. As sleep eased away, Keith realised this was the early-morning sun shining through his eyelids. He breathed in deeply and stretched, feeling the hammock stretch with him, perfectly supporting him. He had slept like a child, returning to deep safety, his body melting away. It was a long time since he'd slept that way, and even longer since he'd woken in the open air, beneath a blue sky.

His fingers groped around for his phone, and then he remembered that he didn't have it.

'How did you sleep?' said a voice.

Ben stood leaning against the gatepost at the entrance to the lumberyard, a few feet from where Keith's hammock was slung. They were in a smallish walled enclosure, full of wood, with a large shed on one side and Ben's cabin at the far end.

'Uh, optimally,' said Keith. His head felt perfectly clear. 'I feel like my operating system was updated in the night.'

'Like what?' said Ben, frowning and smiling.

Keith wondered if he should adjust the way he spoke. He'd been chosen for this assignment because he communicated well with rich people, people at the top. But now he was here he saw that they had shed their sophistication quickly. Perhaps he needed a simpler, pared-down, more inspiring style, like first-term Obama. He felt like he'd had the right tone for a while on the beach yesterday, but it was hard to maintain.

'I slept great,' said Keith. 'Just great. How about you?'

Ben shook his head. 'I have so many worries.' He stared down at the ground, then said, 'You hungry? I have a mango we can share.'

'Sounds great,' said Keith. 'You got any coffee?' And then he mentally kicked himself again, because of course there was no coffee. He really did need to think before he spoke.

To Keith's surprise, Ben said, 'Sure, I've got coffee.' There was a note of pride in his voice.

Ben went into his solid little cabin-house, built on the side of the lumber shed. After a while he came back with two steaming half-coconuts and handed one to Keith.

Keith blew on it gently and took a sip. He smiled appreciatively and nodded to Ben. 'That's good coffee,' he said.

This was a lie. It was horrible, and certainly not coffee. It tasted bitter, gritty and watery, like a heavily diluted tree with a faint coconut aftertaste.

'Can't beat a coffee in the morning,' said Ben. 'Though I have to admit it took me a while to get a taste for it. I guess I'm not as sophisticated as some.'

Keith had moved and was now sitting on a log. The blanket Ben had loaned him was around his shoulders and the sun was pleasantly warm on his back.

'Wait,' said Ben. 'How do you know about coffee? Larry only invented it two weeks ago.'

Keith smiled, waiting for an answer to come to him. What would he say if he had been through the induction protocol like everyone else? In the end, he just shrugged and said, 'I have no idea. I don't know why I know some things but not others. All I really know is that we have to be good to each other.'

Ben looked at him and said, 'I don't know about that. It'd be great if it was that simple.'

They sat in silence for a while, drinking their disgusting coffees. Keith, whose job back in New York required him to appear to enjoy all kinds of vastly expensive unappetising delicacies, from fermented shark to birds' saliva, suffered through it with every trace of satisfaction.

When they'd finished, Ben showed him how to use an axe to strip the bark and smaller branches from a felled tree. Keith was working at this when he heard someone walk through the gateway and stop.

'Oh my gosh,' said a voice. Keith turned and saw the tall thin man with the wayward blond hair – Fifi Maddox. Fifi smiled and blushed, then turned his smile off and on again. 'You're working here now? Oh my gosh. What an … an honour. Do you have any more … messages?'

'Hey, Fifi. No, just the same old message: we need to be kind to folks.' He felt like he was maybe easing into the right tone now.

'You remember my name?' said Fifi, blushing again. 'Wow.'

'Morning, Fifi,' said Ben, emerging with fresh coffees. 'You're on hauling today. You'll be working with Ricky.'

'Sure thing, Ben.'

'You ready for another, big guy?' Ben asked Keith, holding out a steaming half-coconut.

'I would love one,' said Keith. 'But you know what, could you give it to Fifi?'

'Fifi?' said Ben.

Fifi looked from one to the other.

'Excuse me for asking,' said Keith, 'but I'm a very direct person. I appreciate it, Ben, but I can't have two coffees when Fifi's had none. Not when I was just saying we need to be kind to folks.'

After this, Fifi sat and reverently drank the coffee, while Keith got to work trimming the tree trunk. For the first time since he'd been a child, he had a whole project laid out in front of him physically, instead of in a spreadsheet. He could see his progress as he stripped the bark, the axe's blade flat against the trunk. Then he trimmed off any nubs or limbs that protruded, swinging the axe by its handle. He felt the work move through his body instinctively, and marvelled at it, as well as at what a great plyometric workout he was getting here, without having to book a personal-training session at his boutique gym in the Village. The sun shone on his back and he wiped the sweat from his face with his forearm. Looking down, he saw that the beautiful wood, golden and glowing, intricate and alive, was already emerging from the husk of the big felled tree.

When he'd finished, he went to tell Ben, nodding and smiling at the other workers as he passed. Keith found Ben at a table in his cabin, going through figures in a roughly sewn ledger made of banana leaves.

'Finished?' said Ben. 'You can't have. That was two days' work. You've done that in one morning?'

Ben got up and went out into the lumberyard, shielding his eyes against the sun. Keith followed.

'Fifi,' said Ben. 'You're still here? You've been drinking that one coffee all this time?'

Fifi stood up. 'It's my first coffee,' he said, 'and he gave it to me. How long is it supposed to last?'

'Like the time it takes a shadow to grow by two fingers – tops. You mean Ricky has been working on his own all this time? Get out there and help him!'

Fifi slunk out of the gate, muttering something.

Keith said, 'It's my fault. I asked you to give him the coffee.'

Ben frowned and said, 'It's okay. Maybe I'm too hard on him.' Then he asked, 'Hey, if I was too harsh, does that mean I'll have less riches in the United State?'

The next day was the day of rest, which everyone spent doing all the little jobs that had accumulated during the week. Keith slept like a log again, and then woke and swept out the yard. After that, he and Ben shared a mango, and then Ben disappeared into his cabin.

'There's your coffee,' he said when he emerged.

'Thanks a lot,' said Keith, taking the disgusting mixture in its weird hairy cup. 'But it's really not necessary.'

'Hey, you did great work yesterday, and then sweeping today. The least I can do is give you a couple of little luxuries. Like you said, we have to be good to each other.'

Keith took a sip, closed his eyes and turned his face to the sun, as though savouring the taste. In reality, he was trying to put off the next mouthful, while genuinely savouring the sun's warmth on his skin and the pleasant ache in his muscles from yesterday's work. He didn't know how any of them could bear the coffee, and was beginning to suspect that people just instinctively like drinking black stuff from small containers, no matter what it is.

They were standing in the lumberyard near the open gate through which the trees were dragged in and the neatly dressed timbers were shipped out.

'Hi Ricky,' said Ben to a passer-by.

'Hey Ben,' said the man.

'Did Fifi reach you yesterday?'

'Yeah, but it's kind of the same whether he's there or not, you know?'

'Sorry. It was your turn to have him.'

'It's okay,' said Ricky. 'I don't mind.'

'This is Keith,' said Ben.

'Hi,' said Ricky. 'I heard about you – and this message you have. Tell me more about this United State. So we all have like a big house and a million coconuts there?'

Keith suppressed a sigh. 'It's actually more an internal thing. So the key message – I mean, the heart of the message is that we came here to experience love–'

'Love,' said Ricky, looking confused. 'You mean like …' Ricky trailed off, his imagination clearly failing him as he opened and closed his mouth, his eyes blank.

Keith said, 'I mean like, this is my coffee. Right?'

'You have coffee now?' said Ricky to Ben.

'Hey, I'm sophisticated, aren't I?' said Ben. 'I can afford it.'

Keith said, 'Okay, let's stay focused, people – folks, I mean. This is my coffee, untouched, and I'm giving it to you. Because we're all the same. We need to be as good to other folks as we are to ourselves.'

Keith held out the coffee to Ricky.

'You mean it?' said Ricky, taking the cup uncertainly.

'Go ahead. It's yours.'

Ricky took it. He had a large sip, looked from Keith to Ben, and said, 'That's good. Nice brew. Smooth and ... nutty.'

'Right,' said Ben. 'That's what I like about it – the nuttiness.'

'It has excellent texture,' said Keith, who was an expert at lying about how things tasted. 'A very interesting mouthfeel.'

'Yes,' said Ricky, taking another sip. 'The mouthfeel is outstanding.'

He offered it back to Keith, who put up his hands.

'It's great,' said Keith, taking a step back, 'but I don't need it. Just the feel of the sun on my face is enough for me.' This was true: he'd come from the New York winter.

Ricky took another sip and then said, 'Hey, what are you guys doing today? A bunch of us are having a picnic on the Mount.'

'The Mount?' asked Keith.

'Sure. That big hill over there.' He pointed. 'I mean, it's too big to be called a hill, but it's not a mountain, so I guess that's why they call it the Mount. You get a breeze there, and it has great views over the city.'

Keith laughed. He couldn't help it – the idea of these few amateurish shacks being a city.

Ricky and Ben looked at him, eyebrows raised.

'Sorry,' said Keith. 'It wasn't anything. I'm just so happy to … be alive.' He grinned at them, hoping to brazen this out.

Ricky and Ben exchanged a glance, then Ricky laughed.

'You're crazy, man,' he said. 'But you're okay.'

'We're all crazy,' said Keith, 'and we're all okay.'

And they stood in the sun and laughed, and Keith – under the influence of the sun, having escaped the coffee, and two days without email, commuting or diving onto a conference call – realised that he actually was happy to be alive.

Keith and Ben took four mangoes and a couple of bananas to the picnic on the Mount, but on the way they passed the smokehouse and Keith impulsively swapped a mango for three unidentified smoked fish. He was keen to keep his protein intake up, so as not to lose too much of his progress in the gym while he was here. There was no way he was going home with non-ripped abs.

Half the people on the island seemed to be on the Mount that day – half of the workers, anyway. They found Ricky, Fifi and a few others sitting on a cluster of rocks, watching a pair of baby goats playing.

'Keith! Keith!' called Ricky. 'Over here!'

They picked their way over.

'Ooh, fish,' said Fifi, seeing them in their banana-leaf wrapper. 'Can I have some?'

Keith hesitated, but quickly covered it with a smile, remembering that he was meant to be modelling the right behaviour.

'Sure,' he said. 'They're for everyone.'

'Hey, let's all share our food,' said Ricky. 'We're all equal, right? Let's look after each other.'

They ate and chatted, watched the goats play, and looked out, now over the city and now over the sea. People stopped by, greeted each other, stayed to chat. Keith felt that the sun, the perfect breeze and the sound of the waves had between them melted and carried away every bit of tension in his body. He felt perfectly relaxed. There was no phone constantly telling him to attend meetings. All was well.

At some point, Fifi said, 'Do you have anything more to tell us? About your message?'

Ah yes. He was meant to be messaging. But in this moment he felt too relaxed for it. He would get started on it in earnest tomorrow. For now, he needed the rest.

'I'm sorry,' he said, 'but I don't have much to add right now.'

'But what about the United State?' asked Fifi.

'I … misspoke,' said Keith. 'Honestly, forget about that. Just concentrate on here and now.' He stared off out to sea.

'Here and now is all work and worry,' said Ben.

Keith let his eyes close. 'What about *right* here and *right* now?'

'Well, I guess. Yeah, maybe right here and right now is a picnic in the sunshine.'

'What did you mean when you said we came here to experience love?' asked Fifi. 'You mean, like, we should all be making out with each other?'

'No,' said Keith, 'What I mean by love is …'

He trailed off.

He'd had a solid sixty-minute slot to interview Mariko Kami – virtually unprecedented access –

and had crafted with her a very solid script: one core message, plus subsidiary talking points. But now he came down to it, he realised that he wasn't at all sure what she had meant by love.

He stared off, across the sea. He thought of his daughter, Gaia, of how he said he loved her. He remembered bringing her back from the hospital, only a year or so ago, this tiny shrunken red thing, and how he … had actually, really, felt nothing in particular. He had said he had, but he hadn't. But what did he feel about her now, more than a year later? How did he feel when she swayed clumsily over to him, like a tiny drunkard, on her stumpy little legs, and silently raised her chubby little arms for him to pick her up?

For the first time it hit him that his daughter was no longer just part of a life project at which he was trying to out-compete all the other parents he knew. When she raised her little arms and he put his hands on her sides and picked her up, and she fitted into him just above his hip, it felt like they were both the same thing: not him and her, but the same. And it felt good then. It felt good. There was no way of saying more than that.

He realised he was not going to be able to explain love. Not right now. First he needed to recover from having genuinely experienced it. He looked out at them, at the people all around him, seeing that they too were children. And they looked back.

Fifi said, 'These fish are surprisingly filling, aren't they?'

'Totally,' said Ricky. 'It looked like there would no way be enough for all of us.'

5

THE WAY IT IS

It was fifteen days since Keith had arrived, and Peter had gathered together the most influential citizens in his new third-floor meeting room.

Tom – sitting in front of the window through which his own four-floor house could be seen – gave a broad, insultingly relaxed smile and leaned back a little further in his chair.

'Peter, I remember the first time we spoke, when you told me a fairy tale about how dangerous the forest is, and how I'd need to give you my blanket to make it worth your while to brave the terrible dangers lurking there.'

The others in the room stopped talking and grinned uneasily. Bodies shifted on wooden furniture, making it creak, despite the special joints that Larry had designed. Hands clenched around the rough hair of the coconut cups. Luke, who owned the paper workshop, caught the eye of Elmer, who had built the new floor on Peter's house. Matthew, who was in the ink business, looked at the floor. Abigail, the goose-farmer, tapped her teeth and glanced at Simon, who owned the fishing-boat. And Ben, who owned the lumberyard, took a deep draught of coffee and looked at the table. Tom's secretary, the beautiful Susan, sitting on a stool just behind his chair, was far too tense and composed to allow her expression to change. And Wayne, Tom's security man, was almost as limited in his range of facial movements as Barrel, who stood beside him at the door.

Peter, still proud of this early masterstroke, sat back and let out a loud laugh. 'Ha! That's right. Have you scraped the coconuts together to buy a new one yet?'

Tom laughed too – deliberately, as though he were speaking the words 'ha, ha, ha' – and the others joined in more quietly. 'I have plenty of blankets, Peter. Don't you worry about me. And please don't apologise,' he said, as though Peter had.

Peter took a sip of his coffee and said, 'In this life nobody's going to do anything for you, so you got to help yourself, make your own luck. The only rule is, a deal's a deal. Make an agreement with someone and you've got to keep it, no matter what. Now maybe that's not what Keith's going around saying, but that's my rule.'

'It most certainly is not what Keith's "going around saying". And that's why I called this meeting...'

'*You* called this meeting? It was *me*, you...' Peter stopped and looked at Tom, who was clearly trying to needle him. 'Anyway, it's not important. What's important is that we've got ourselves a situation and we need to take action.'

'By the way, is it true you took Keith's backpack?' asked Tom.

'Sure. He said it wasn't important. I wanted to show him it is. It can get cold at night without a blanket. And you can get to stink if you don't change your underwear once in a while. Maybe that's not the case in this magic "United State" he talks about...'

Simon leaned forward. 'Actually, he seems kind of annoyed about that. Like it's a secret he shouldn't have mentioned.'

'Hooey,' said Peter. 'He might walk around all humble but he only mentions what he means to mention.'

'But …' It was Ben, the lumberyard owner, who wore a moustache and whose hair was on the long side, who had spoken. When he saw their eyes were on him he stopped, as though he had said the word involuntarily.

'Yes?'

'Well. Keith isn't so bad. He always turns up on time for his shift at my lumberyard, and if there's work to be done he stays longer. He's one of the best workers I've got. He's not interested in being paid, and if I try to give him anything – purely for incentive, you understand – he gives it away.'

The door opened and Angela walked in with a fresh round of coffees on a wooden tray. She looked at Peter and opened her mouth to say something.

'On the table, Angela! On the table.'

She set it down apologetically, almost spilling the coffee, then rushed back to the door. Her footsteps sank down the stairs.

'Rumour has it,' said Tom, 'that *she's* one of them.'

'Angela? A Keithian?' said Peter. 'No way. She's too smart.'

Tom raised his eyebrows insinuatingly. There was a silence.

'But I can't deny he's got everyone talking,' said Peter. 'It's because he just appeared like that, so long after the rest of us. Suddenly it's all, "Where did we come from? Why are we here? What comes next?"'

There were nods around the table. Peter glanced around, smiled and continued. 'I tell them the answers every day: "Nowhere. No particular reason. Nothing." But people are dumb. They won't accept the obvious answers. The bullshit distracts them. The truth is, you've got to work hard on this island if you want a ...'

He gestured around him, his hand encompassing the house, the view, the closed ledgers and the key to the strongroom.

Tom finished his sentence for him, glancing ostentatiously out of the east window, where his own house could be seen. 'A *four*-floor house?'

Everyone laughed and Peter had to force a smile.

'Next month,' said Peter, nodding at Elmer. 'Next month. And you know who Keith's message really appeals to? *Losers*. If you got nothing, it's great to hear this guy with the nice hair tell you fairy tales about how you'll be rich in the United State.'

'He can't quite make up his mind though, can he?' said Tom. 'He said that when you leave, each moment you spent here will seem as precious as coconut milk when you've been working outside all morning – whatever *that* feels like.'

They all laughed again, the ones who worked indoors more loudly than those like Ben whose skin was dark and hands calloused.

'But then there's all that piffle about how everything we've got here is as nothing compared with the riches waiting for us in the United State. Honestly, which is it – precious or worthless?'

'Long story short: the guy's a jerk,' said Peter.

'Speaking for myself,' said Tom, 'I'm confident that I could ignore a long-hair talking nonsense. What I find difficult to overlook is the effect on productivity. Have any of you found that your profits have been adversely impacted?'

'Maybe,' said Peter. The others looked at the floor, then raised their heads and met each other's eyes. There were slow nods.

'A couple of days ago,' said Simon, 'my crew

went off to the lumberyard to talk to Keith, instead of doing their shift. They said we had enough fish for the moment.'

'He works well himself at my lumberyard,' said Ben, 'but the others slack off more since he's come.'

'My ink workers' productivity has fallen in the last week,' said Matthew. 'It was a mystery, but now I know why.

'So what do we do about it?' said Abigail, the goose farmer.

Tom put his coffee cup down with a thud. 'Peter,' he said, 'you raised an interesting point earlier.'

'I did?' said Peter, looking around the room in cynical mock-delight and making the others laugh.

'Strange as it may seem, yes. You said, "Once you've made a deal, you've got to stick to it." And if someone fails to stick to a deal, well then a new deal comes into force. And that new deal is that someone else – Barrel, say, or Wayne – will come around and have a word, and that word will hurt.'

'Right,' said Peter. 'That's the way it is.'

'We all stick to the way it is, don't we?' asked Tom. There were nods. 'We all uphold the way it is. And we all, between us, and with a couple of large friends, enforce the way it is.'

'Right again,' said Peter.

'So, what if a person doesn't go against the way it is himself – perhaps he turns up for his shift at, say, the lumberyard on time every day – can he not, nonetheless, be responsible for the fact that other people are contravening the way it is?'

'You're saying that if some fishermen disobey the way it is because they heard some bullshit about a United State, then the person who talked the bullshit has disobeyed the way it is,' said Peter.

'In a nutshell, yes,' said Tom. 'I mean, isn't it just as bad to make someone else violate the way it is, as to violate it oneself?'

'Worse,' said Peter.

'So, why would we fail to punish that?' asked Tom. 'People look to us to enforce the way it is, for everyone's benefit. And here we have someone openly flouting the way it is – and we do nothing?'

'That son of a bitch!' said Peter.

'We need to take action,' said Matthew.

'Then let us do so,' said Tom, and looked at Peter.

A group of them – Peter, Barrel, Luke, Matthew and Simon – waited in the lumberyard's main building. It was twilight and the building was dark, so they couldn't be seen by those out in the open yard. Peter swapped his stick from hand to hand and quietly scuffed his feet in the bare earth of the floor, wondering whether this was the right time. From the yard, full of logs and planks, came the sharp, sweet smell of sap, livening the cool room.

He watched the men in the yard as they ate, drank and talked, sitting around a great chunk of tree that was mounted on trestles. There were thirteen of them, with Ben and Keith sitting side by side. They were using the tree as a table, eating off the rough bark. No doubt soon it would be cut into smaller pieces and finished. The men were laughing, drinking from coconuts that had been left open for a while so that the milk fermented.

'You do the honours, Keith,' said Ben, the lumberyard owner.

Keith stood and made a toast. 'To trees and love,' he said, raising his coconut shell. He took a gulp and then handed it to the man on his left.

'Okay then,' said his neighbour, '"to trees and love". You're crazy, man.' He took a swallow and passed it left again. Meanwhile, Keith hacked open a mango and passed the pieces around to the right. Ben took one and ate it messily.

Peter whispered, 'Ben said he was going to send Keith in here, damn it. Seems like he's fallen under his spell instead.'

'Give him time,' said Luke.

'Time? He's already had the length of that shadow. It's grown by the size of my foot while we've been waiting. I think he's lost his nerve. Well, we haven't lost ours, have we?'

He stared at each of them in turn. They shook their heads.

'Right,' said Peter.

He stepped into the lumberyard. 'Hi, Ben. It's your favourite customer, Peter.'

The men sitting around their improvised table turned to look at him.

'Hello, Peter,' said Ben, awkwardly, rising to his feet.

There was a moment of silence.

'Peter,' said Keith, standing up and smiling. 'Take my chair, take a load off. Come on, we're in a lumberyard. We can find a few more bits of wood to sit on.'

'Very kind, thanks,' said Peter. 'But we'd like to

talk to you in my house. It's more comfortable. There's a few things we'd like your advice on.'

'Sure,' said Keith. 'How about tomorrow night? Ben arranged a lumberyard supper for tonight.'

Keith was still smiling, but the other lumberyard workers had stood and were eyeing Peter and his friends.

One of the workers said to Peter, 'You aren't his friend. What are you here for?'

'We can all be friends,' said Keith, keeping his smile nice and relaxed, though there was a tension around his eyes.

'You heard him,' said Peter. 'We can all be friends. We just want to love Keith, like everyone else.'

'So what are the sticks for?'

'Help us walk. Our feet get tired.'

'I don't know why you get tired,' said the lumberyard worker. 'You don't work.'

'Hey!' shouted Peter. 'I work four times as hard as you, moron. I was up half the night and then back to work at dawn. How'd do you think I earned my three floors?'

'Moron?' said the worker. 'Come on then!' The man pushed his chair out of the way and squared up to Peter.

'Sure, hit me,' said Peter. 'I guess you don't want to keep your job.'

Peter looked meaningfully at Ben, who said, 'Ricky …'

The worker swung at Peter, but his timing was off, allowing Peter to dodge so that the fumbled blow caught his ear instead of his jaw.

The next moment, the worker was on the floor, felled by a blow from Barrel's stick. He stayed down, not moving.

'Grab Keith!' shouted Peter.

Barrel dropped his stick and held Keith in a bear hug.

'Hey, what are you doing?' said Ben.

'You know what we're doing,' said Peter. 'Don't try to wheedle your way out of it now. You planned this with us, remember?'

'We didn't say anything about sticks. Christ, look at Ricky.'

Ricky was still lying on the floor, blood trickling from his temple. He stirred but didn't get up.

'He'll come around. Now tell those guys to sit down. We're leaving. I want to have our little talk now, Keith.'

'Sit down,' said Keith to the lumberyard

workers. 'I'll go with them. You can let go of me, Barrel. Just let me check on Ricky.'

Ben's workers looked angry, afraid, disoriented. Ben glanced at them, at Keith, at Peter and the men with sticks. He spread his arms, making a calming gesture with his hands.

'Sit down, boys,' said Ben. 'It's what he wants. We can't stand up to them.'

They sat, reluctantly, not meeting each other's eyes.

Barrel looked at Peter, who nodded. Keith, suddenly freed from his grip, crouched down beside Ricky, who was now lying on his back.

'Can you hear me?' he asked, taking Ricky's hand away from his temple so he could look at the wound. The side of Ricky's head was swollen already and the skin was broken.

Ricky groaned and nodded his head, wincing.

Keith stood and moved for the table, but found Barrel blocking his path.

'He needs water,' said Keith.

'Bring that water bottle,' said Peter to Luke, pointing at the table.

Luke handed the water bottle to Ricky, who was sitting up now, leaning against a stack of wood. He drank deeply, then put his hand gingerly to his temple again.

'What the …?' Ricky finally said.

'You messed with us,' said Peter. 'We don't like that. You messed with The Way It Is.'

Keith gave a forced laugh. 'To go to all this trouble, this must be one hell of a conversation you guys want to have with me.'

'Oh, it is,' said Peter. 'We want to talk about the meaning of life.'

6

SEND HIM BACK

From the walled lumberyard, they had taken Keith to the upstairs room of Matthew's ink shop. Someone had put a blanket over his head for the journey and, as arranged, Tom and Wayne had set light to a bonfire on the Mount, to create a distraction. True, the lumberyard workers would spread word of what had happened, but so long as no one knew where Keith was, Peter didn't mind being unpopular. After all, popular didn't pay the bills.

Hours had passed, and dawn was now lighting the edges of the sky. Keith's guilt was obvious; the punishment was not.

Peter said it again. 'We've got to do something

that'll get rid of this trouble once and for all, something that'll put an end to his mischief.'

'Take him to the other side of the island?' someone suggested.

'Where we can't even keep our eyes on him?' said Peter.

They were tired. A silence fell over them.

Peter was rocking on his stool, sipping at a cold coffee. 'If only he'd never come. If only we could make it like he'd never come.'

'Perhaps we could,' said Tom, reclining in a chair nearby. Peter had thought he was asleep. 'Perhaps we could send him back to where he came from.'

'What do you mean?' asked Peter, suspiciously.

'I don't know. I'm just thinking aloud here. I mean, he came out of the ocean. Why don't we send him back there? Take a fishing boat, tie him to a raft, tow him out to sea and cast him adrift.'

'We don't have a raft.'

'I do. It's on the beach. I was going to experiment with a new way of fishing, but I'll gladly donate it.'

'But who'd do it?'

'I don't know. Wayne's sick. It'd have to be someone with plenty of guts.'

Peter stood up and walked over to the window. The sky was glowing, huge, standing over the dark sea, staining it red. His mind was spinning. He hadn't slept. His body was clammy with sweat. The same loop of thought kept running around his head. It was a big step, sending someone back out into the sea. And what if it backfired? What if everyone rose up, refused to work, took stuff that wasn't theirs? What if people stopped obeying The Way It Is?

On the other hand, everything was so close to being in his grasp. He was negotiating with Elmer to build two storeys at once, overtaking Tom. His control of lobsters and clams were finally shifting the balance of power his way. This was his moment.

Another wave of tiredness hit him. He took another sip of his cold coffee. It smelled dusty, sharp, burnt. He sniffed at it, then at his shirt. The smell was stronger now. It wasn't him or the coffee but something else in the room. He looked around, then stood up.

'Fire!'

It was a shout from outside in the street. The shout came again, and suddenly the people in the room were waking, or roused from their dozing thoughts, and shaking their neighbours by the shoulder. They moved to the window nearest the shout.

Tom remained sitting. 'What should we do?' he asked, looking to Peter.

Peter glanced over at Keith, who had passed out in his chair, his gag still in his mouth, breathing loudly through his nose. They didn't need to worry about him for the moment, at least while Peter took charge of the fire. He walked over to the window, where Luke stood staring out into the street.

'Oh my God, Peter!' said Luke.

'What?' asked Peter.

'Look!'

And then he could see it. Flames, long and angry, were licking at the sky. It was Luke's sun deck, burning. He was gratified to see that it was still dwarfed by his own three storeys behind it.

But then he saw it wasn't Luke's sun deck. It was beyond that.

Peter dashed out of the door and into the street. He could hear Barrel behind him. He ran up the street, along by the beach, rounded the corner by Luke's, and then he saw it. Then he knew it.

His house. His beautiful house.

The whole of the ground floor was aflame. And the tongues of fire were climbing, snakes of flame flinging themselves upward, licking at the panelling of the second storey, falling back, renewing the effort, catching hold, these flames burning and eating, upward, consuming his house.

'Peter!'

He turned. It was Angela, running to him. Her arms were around him.

'Peter, thank God! I thought you were inside!' She was crying.

'Never mind that. Why weren't *you* inside?'

'Peter, it's dawn,' she said, struggling to stop crying, wiping away the tears. 'I was at my shack, sleeping. I just saw it now.'

'Sleeping! You idiot, Angela! My house! My goddamn house! Get a bucket! Get water!'

'I don't think we can put it out, Peter. It's reached the third floor.'

Peter ran to the door. The heat was scorching, overwhelming. He kicked the door, which flapped in, engulfed. Peter glimpsed the staircase collapsing, the ceiling bowing in, and then a burst of heat roared out, knocking him off his feet.

It was hopeless. His house was gone.

He crawled away from the devouring heat, and

a wave of hatred flowed through him. *Keith.* That son of a bitch. His followers had done this.

Peter had crawled far enough away from the fire now. He felt his skin cooling. It felt raw and damaged. He got to his feet and, ignoring whatever Angela was saying, ran back to Matthew's ink shop.

He knocked on the door and Matthew opened it, looking alarmed.

'Are you all right? Your face is black!'

Peter put a hand to his face. It came away dark and sooty, and his fingertips told him that he'd lost his eyebrows. He looked down and noticed that the hairs on the backs of his hands had crisped and caramelised, reduced to crumbly bobbles of carbon.

'I'm going to carry out the sentence right now.'

'Are you sure? Why don't you sit down, take a bath?'

But Tom was there beside Matthew, laying a hand on his shoulder and drawing him aside.

'Peter's right,' said Tom. 'This needs doing now, while he's got the will.'

'Damn right, I've got the will.'

'Where did you say that raft was, Tom?' asked Peter.

'Down on the beach. It's already tied to a boat.'

At that moment, Barrel came panting up behind Peter.

'Right,' said Peter. 'Come on, Barrel. Give me my backpack, and grab Keith.'

Barrel handed over Peter's rucksack. Then Tom stood aside and Barrel shouldered his way into the room, picked up the sleeping Keith, chair and all, and set off for the beach.

'Wait,' said Peter. He took a blanket off the bed and draped it over Keith, who was awake now, wide-eyed and struggling. 'We don't want anyone seeing him.'

They hurried down to the beach, ignoring the stares of the few people who were not looking at the burning remains of Peter's house. Most of them were too distracted by their desire to see what was going on in town to pay much attention to the two figures making for the beach, one black with soot, the other carrying a blanketed burden.

At the beach, they removed the blanket and set to work quickly, untying a limb at a time and immediately securing it to the edges of the little raft, which could almost have been tailor-made for him.

And then they dragged the boat down to the

water, with Keith on his raft trailing behind. Peter pushed the boat out and jumped in, grabbed the oars and started rowing. The water soaked Keith's clothes, but lifted the raft up. It bobbed out to sea, towed behind the boat by the short length of rope.

'Take off the gag now!' called Peter.

Barrel struggled into the waves, the water up to his waist, and removed the gag from Keith's mouth. Keith called out – a wordless, indistinct sound, which soon gave way to spluttering as seawater sloshed over him. Peter heaved at the oars and the boat pulled out, leaving the shore further and further behind.

'Now you'll see what happens when you burn my house down!' he shouted.

Keith spat out the water and shouted something back, but Peter didn't hear it. 'No possessions, huh?' shouted Peter. 'Well now you got no possessions! And you wanted to take everything I had too!'

He stopped shouting and put his energy into rowing, straining against the water with his oars. There was silence apart from Peter's loud grunting as he fought his way through the water and Keith's coughing and spitting and gasping as he fought for breath.

* * *

Peter had been rowing for a long time. He had poured his fury into it. Now he stopped and mopped his brow with one sleeve. He was soaked with seawater and sweat, and streaked with liquid black soot. The sun was well up above the horizon. Clouds bunched timidly in the distance, beyond the island. And into this silence Keith spoke.

'You know, if you do this, Peter, you'll be really disappointed with yourself!'

'Oh yeah?'

'You'll regret it!'

'What, when I get judged by the Grand Fairy in the magical United State?'

'United States! States! Don't you remember it?'

'Sure, just like I remember the Happy Land of Figs.'

'Listen, the United States is a real place, just like here – except more complicated, with more people, more stuff – it's a country. And you *could* get judged there, by an actual judge, for attempted murder if you set me adrift. Untie me now and the corporation won't go to the cops.'

'What are the *cops?*'

'Sort of like a whole bunch of Barrels.'

'Right. You're crazy.'

There was a short silence as Keith spat out some seawater.

'Still with this serene act, huh?' said Peter.

'You know what?' shouted Keith. 'Just set me adrift.'

'What?'

'Set me adrift! We're being monitored. I'll bob around on the waves for a while until you get far enough away, and then a boat or a helicopter will pick me up. I'll go back to the United States. And then I'll quit my job, spend *way* more time with my wife and kid, maybe move to the country, *definitely* stop going to strip clubs. I'm going to do better. I'm going to be more like Keith – just work my shifts, be a good guy and sleep well at night. I liked it.'

'Does all that still happen if I turn the raft over?'

Keith was silent. Peter looked over at him and saw that his eyes were wide open in panic and that he was struggling against the ropes that held him.

Peter laughed. 'Not so serene now, huh?'

'Please don't do that, Peter. If you turn the raft over I'll die. I'll drown. You can't have forgotten about death!'

'So what happens if you die, Keith?'

'I don't know. I don't want to find out! I'm young – I've got a kid!'

Peter rowed again in silence, a grim look on his face. After a while he said, 'Do you know how *hard* I worked for that house you burned down? For all those coconuts?'

'Yes,' said Keith.

'Yes? *Yes?* How would you know?'

'Fourteen-hour days, minimum. Headaches. Sleepless nights. Feeling like you're going blind with work. Stomach cramps. And then you see other people sunning themselves between shifts, laughing in the evenings – and you're missing out on it all, just because you know you can do better.'

There was a short silence.

'Okay,' said Peter. 'I guess you do know. I don't know how. And you still burned it down?'

'I was locked up. How could I burn it down?'

'You know what I mean – your people did it.'

'I have no people. And if they were really "my people" they'd have left it alone. I didn't want people to burn stuff – I just wanted everyone to love each other – my bonus depended on it.'

'Your bonus?' He stopped. 'Wait a minute.'

'What?'

'Son of a bitch!' shouted Peter.

And then Keith started laughing: an unhinged, manic laughter that came from nowhere.

'You know what?' Keith shouted. 'At this point I can handle being called a son of a bitch.'

'Not you. Tom. Goddamn son-of-a-bitch Tom. I've been set up.'

Keith laughed again. 'You think you've been set up! I'm tied to a raft here! I'm going to be drowned – for my stupid piece-of-shit job kissing up to rich guys. When I think of what I wanted to be when I was a kid …'

'There's no way in hell I'm going to let Tom manoeuvre me into drowning the most popular guy on the island. He burned my house down to make me mad enough to do this. Well I'm the only one who had the guts to do it, and I'm the only one who has the guts *not* to do it. I'd like to see his face when I come back. "Hi Tom. I had a moment of revelation and saved the life of the island saint, and he says we should all get rid of all our property. Let's start with yours." Goddamn! Let's see how he likes losing *his* house.'

Peter stopped rowing and pulled on the rope that connected the boat to the raft.

'What're you doing?' asked Keith, his voice leaping up two octaves and breaking.

'Don't worry. I'm setting you free.'

Peter took off his rucksack, pulled out the axe and set to work, using the blade to slice through the knots at Keith's ankles.

'Careful not to shift your weight,' said Peter. 'We don't want to overturn the raft.'

'You know,' said Keith, 'to be honest, I'd rather you just set me adrift. I'll be picked up in five minutes. I could be back in the United States tomorrow.'

'Are you still on with this United State bullshit? You're coming back with me. I'm telling you, the island is all there is – the rest is just in your mind.'

When he had untied Keith and got him back into the boat, Peter began to row back to the island, towing the now-empty raft behind them.

7

JUST WHY?

Mariko looked down at her hands in her lap and silently ordered her fists to unclench. When she glanced up, Ellory was looking expectantly at Josh, signalling him to continue.

'So,' said Josh, who had been called Keith, 'once we got back to shore, there were a lot of people waiting on the beach – practically the whole island. They looked like they wanted to kill Peter. But then they saw that I was safe, and Peter started speaking.'

'What did he say?' asked Mr Mori.

'That was when he began his operation against Tom – just like he'd told me on the raft – because he was convinced that Tom had ordered the fire that destroyed his house.'

'And you believe this also?' asked Ellory.

'It's plausible,' said Josh, 'maybe even most likely. Peter was not a popular guy at that point, but I can't see anyone burning his house down, not at that stage. Maybe I'm wrong, but I think a lot of people remembered, at some level, why they had come there.'

Ellory nodded and fitted his cigar back into his mouth.

'So Peter started speaking,' repeated Josh. 'He told them he had wanted to teach me a lesson, because he'd been so full of grief about losing everything. He said he'd taken me out to sea to scare me, but that there had been a great storm and a blinding light, and then he had seen that I was right, and that he was glad he'd lost everything. He said he'd seen that we shouldn't be building up riches on the island, because what we had was as nothing compared with … with the United State.'

'The amnesia had worn off?' asked Mr Mori.

'No, it … Well, I guess it doesn't matter, since … But, yeah, I slipped up right when I first arrived and mentioned the US, but they misheard it as the United State, like it was Nirvana or something. And …' He trailed off.

'And?' said Ellory gently, after a few seconds.

'And that was when Peter basically persuaded everyone – or a bunch of people – to burn down Tom's house and take all his stuff.'

'Persuaded them how?'

'Well, I had said, you know, that we were all equal – basically the messaging we agreed on in advance of the intervention – and that we needed to stop focusing on material things and status ...'

He paused, as though gathering his thoughts. He glanced at the universe of pale fish in their gargantuan tank, the Redwood conference table, the view over New York. 'And, of course, that we came here to experience love. But he really went all in on this equality part of it. And I was right there saying, "No, it's the love part, focus on that." But Peter was saying, "Love means equality," and he seemed to be agreeing with me, but actually ... Well, anyway, quite a lot of people went over to Tom's house and–'

'You went along?' asked Ellory.

'No, I wanted to show I had nothing to do with it. But of course they said they were doing Keith's work – you know my name there was Keith?'

They nodded.

'And Tom came out, apparently, and said he'd been planning on giving half of his possessions to support my work. But there was this chant of "All of it, all of it". And yeah, so that happened. They burned it down.'

'And this was when the real difficulties began, was it not?' said Mr Mori.

'Yeah, so that was the week of the house burnings. People were saying, "We need to become equal, no matter how painful that is." And I was saying, "No, you're already equal and that's why you need to stop making everything so painful by burning people's houses down."'

'And just to be clear, you were still staying away from the house burnings?' said Mr Mori.

'No, by this point I was right there telling them not to burn the houses down.'

'They didn't listen?'

'They listened, but they would just wink at me and say, "We know what you mean."'

'Wasn't there anyone truly listening to you?' asked Mr Mori.

'There were some, but they just became another faction adding to the chaos. Angela wrote this allegorical short story about the whole situation, but it didn't really change anything.'

'And then?'

'And then things calmed down a little, but I

don't know what would have happened if it had carried on. Thankfully, a day or so later time was up, and you did your thing with the gas in the night and the reintegration experience, so …'

'So. Thank you very much, Josh,' said Mr Mori.

'We're grateful,' said Ellory. 'Could it be that you will think again?' He waved his hand at a letter that lay on the table.

'Thanks a lot, Mr Ellory,' said Josh. 'And I am grateful for this opportunity, truly, and for your kind offer to let me stay on, but … I'm out. I like working with wood, and I want to spend time with my kid.'

'You know we wish you all the best?' said Ellory.

Josh nodded. Then he stood, shook hands with Ellory, who remained seated, and Mr Mori, who stood. He did a sort of half-bow towards Mariko, and left the room.

Mariko heard the door close behind him. She put her hands over her face, just for a moment, and then lowered them, her expression neutral, waiting to see what would come next.

'Miss Kami,' said Mr Mori, sitting forward. He had turned down the smile on his neat face to its lowest setting. 'Events have not transpired as we would have wished–'

'No,' she said emphatically.

'And yet when I read the transcripts of the debriefing interviews, it is not such a negative picture.'

She looked at him.

'Those who were not rich on the island,' he said, 'report overwhelmingly that they learned a great deal and are grateful for the experience. David Moss, for example, head technologist of DelphiSoft, known on the island as "Larry" – and incidentally by far the richest of our islanders in the real world – said the experience was "neat".'

'*Neat?*' said Mariko. 'What more did he say?'

Mr Mori flipped through a stapled document. 'Uh, not a great deal. Mr Moss is not an excessively expressive individual. But he gave the overall experience a rating of nine out of ten, and circled the terms "learning" and "bonding" on the feedback sheet.'

Mariko looked at Ellory, but he simply smoked his cigar, eyes closed.

'Dorothy R Lebus, or "Angela", author of the bestselling *Feverwell* books, said, "I have now seen poverty, exploitation and injustice at first hand,

and know that I can survive it. I'm ready to start living in a more courageous and loving way". Fifi Maddox, son of rock legend Brian Maddox, said he was "humbled and awestruck by the amazing experience." Chazz Darles, realtor, known as "Barrel", said it was "awesome". Ceecee Quinn, owner of the wellness brand Quince, and known on the island as "Susan", said "my days and nights cracked me open like an egg and brought me to the next level of conscience."'

'What does this mean?' asked Mariko.

'We're not entirely sure, but it is positive. She rated the experience a seven out of ten.'

Mariko shook her head. She was distressed that all her work, all her excitement at this idea, had turned into these ratings and reviews, even the best of which seemed to have missed the point.

'And those who were not poor on the island?'

'A … more mixed experience,' said Mr Mori. 'George F. Crocket, or "Ben", an oilman and rancher based outside of Houston, Texas, said, "I have learned that I am capable, out of fear and greed, of betraying a good man and a friend. I will be making changes, and the world will see that I can be a different and better sort of man." He rated the experience a nine.'

'This is good,' said Mariko. 'He understood.'

'Indeed,' said Mr Mori. 'Most gratifying. However …'

He stopped, took a breath and glanced at Ellory, who nodded, eyes still closed.

'However?' asked Mariko.

'Seven of the nine wealthiest individuals – assessed in terms of estimated coconut holdings at the time the burnings began – are currently taking legal advice about a possible class-action suit against us.'

'Why?'

'We won't know unless and until the suit is served, but through talking to people who have talked to people, the substance seems to be' – he took a second document from the table and read from the first page – 'that, by providing an environment that allowed them to become rich, Elcor deprived them of the chance to experience love, which was what they had paid for, thus putting us in breach of contract. Also trauma from having their houses burned down.'

'They want their money back?' asked Mariko. 'But they pay not so much, for such rich people.'

'The indications are that they would be seeking substantial damages.'

Mariko took a white silk handkerchief from her small lacquered purse and put it to her face, needing the calming feel of silk against her skin.

'Peter is behind this?' she asked.

'Actually, it seems the instigator was Steven Ignatieff, manager of the alternative investments fund True Alpha, known on the island as "Tom".'

'But Peter is one of them.'

'Actually, Peter – real name Alan Peterson, almost making him the second person on the island to be correctly named – has said that he is prepared to testify in our favour. As he was the island's richest individual, this would gravely weaken their case.'

Mariko looked at Mr Mori, eyes wide. She was surprised, but she sensed there was more.

'Why does he not join them?' she asked. 'It would make him still richer, if they win. He is also a businessman, I suppose.'

'Actually, no,' said Mr Mori. 'Peterson works on a part-time basis for E-Z Limos in New Jersey.'

'Then how did he …?'

'He won his place in a competition, though he was not the target audience. Apparently, he found out about it in a copy of *Lifestyle Therapist* magazine, which was left in the back of his car. We were legally not allowed to restrict entry to the competition.'

'So,' she said.

'Peterson has a condition,' said Mr Mori, 'for not joining the lawsuit.'

'What is that?'

'He would like to meet you, Miss Kami.'

She took a breath, unclenched her fists. 'I cannot meet this man. He has destroyed everything.'

'Can you see, Kami San,' said Ellory, eyes now open, voice seeming to bubble up through the floor, 'that I would appreciate this favour?'

* * *

They had withdrawn, leaving Mariko alone in the huge board room. She was looking out of the window. It was a windy day and a bank of cloud was trawling a shadow over the city, so that the buildings shone as they emerged.

Behind her, the door clicked open.

She turned, and in walked a man: bald, lightly tanned, with bags under his eyes, wearing a baggy black suit. He walked the length of the room, glancing around, and then lowered himself stiffly into the chair opposite her.

He made a gesture that took in the view, the table and the vast aquarium, and said, 'Nice place, if you like fish.'

'You wish to speak with me, I think,' she said, turning to the tray beside her and pouring coffees from a tall silver jug into eggshell-blue cups. She could not bear to look at him.

'Yes I do,' he said.

'Please. Go on.' She looked at the surface of her coffee, seeing from its smooth inky surface that her hand was not shaking.

She heard him sigh and pause. She looked up.

'Why?' he said.

'Why what?' she asked.

'I don't know,' he said. He seemed tired. 'Just why? Why does everything hurt? Why did you set it up that way? Why didn't you protect me from myself?'

'But how could I have known you would behave so badly and make yourself so miserable?'

'Because I'm a human being,' he said.

'Yes. This is difficult. Sorry.'

'You know something? I'm a multiple-bankrupt and a part-time budget limo driver and I live with my *mom*. Maybe you didn't know that. I'm fifty-six and I had to move back in with my eighty-year-old mom because I can't make it.'

She didn't say anything. She was holding her white handkerchief tightly.

'I've started nine companies in my life,' he said, 'and every one has failed. Bad luck, I guess, or maybe I just ride people too hard.'

She nodded.

'I didn't even enter that competition,' he said. 'I brought that magazine in from the car and my mom found it and entered for me. And when I won, I figured, "What the heck – free beach holiday."'

Mariko again looked at the surface of the coffee, now covered in little ripples.

'And then I get there,' he said, 'and finally – after all those years trying – I become rich. I'm rich. And it's just coconuts. It's just goddamn coconuts. And worse: I now know for a fact that getting rich won't even make me happy. And I also know that making everyone else poor won't make me happy.'

'This is true. Sorry.' And she did, suddenly, feel sorry for him, bitter and abrasive as he was. And she was sorry for herself too: rich and lonely and finding so much so difficult to bear.

'And so I'm left with nothing,' he said.

'Yes,' she agreed.

There was a silence.

She looked up at him and said, 'Why have you come here?'

'Because I wanted to tell you ...' He stopped and looked out of the window, across the vast crammed richness of New York. And then he glanced back at her, almost shyly, caught her eye and said, 'Maybe it's enough.' He looked down at his lap, at his empty hands. 'Maybe nothing is plenty.'

THE END

ALSO BY CHRISTOPHER SHEVLIN

The Perpetual Astonishment of Jonathon Fairfax

Jonathon Fairfax Must Be Destroyed

The Spy Who Came in from the Bin

Website

christophershevlin.com